Cover Copy

Traveling through time…for a Highlander.

Anne MacLeod's identical ancestor has made a wish on the Fairy Flag at Dunvegan Castle, one which sees the two young women swapping places in time and leaving Anne set to handfast with the very man her ancestor wished to escape. Only Anne sees the possibilities, because now she could change the future and ensure her parents never perished in the inferno which took their lives.

Highland warrior Alex MacDonald has made an agreement to handfast with Anne in order to bring a halt to the feud raging between their clans. The last thing he expects though is a woman claiming to come from the future, a woman who stirs him on a physical and emotional level to protect, and to even believe.

When Anne finds herself in her MacLeod chief's presence, she chooses to go with him in order to leave a message for her parents. In full pursuit, Alex wages a battle of the heart, and of the very essence of time. Can he defy the odds as Anne is taken from him…to work his own magic and get her back?

Books by Joanne Wadsworth

The Matheson Brothers Series
Highlander's Desire, Book One
Highlander's Passion, Book Two
Highlander's Seduction, Book Three
Highlander's Kiss, Book Four
Highlander's Heart, Book Five
Highlander's Sword, Book Six
Highlander's Bride, Book Seven
Highlander's Caress, Book Eight
Highlander's Touch, Book Nine
Highlander's Shifter, Book Ten
Highlander's Claim, Book Eleven
Highlander's Courage, Book Twelve
Highlander's Mermaid, Book Thirteen

Highlander Heat Series
Highlander's Castle, Book One
Highlander's Magic, Book Two
Highlander's Charm, Book Three
Highlander's Guardian, Book Four
Highlander's Faerie, Book Five
Highlander's Champion, Book Six
Highlander's Captive (Short Story)

Billionaire Bodyguards Series
Billionaire Bodyguard Attraction, Book One
Billionaire Bodyguard Boss, Book Two
Billionaire Bodyguard Fling, Book Three

Books by Joanne Wadsworth

Regency Brides Series
The Duke's Bride, Book One
The Earl's Bride, Book Two
The Wartime Bride, Book Three
The Earl's Secret Bride, Book Four
The Prince's Bride, Book Five
Her Pirate Prince, Book Six

Princesses of Myth Series
Protector, Book One
Warrior, Book Two
Hunter (Short Story - Included in Warrior, Book Two)
Enchanter, Book Three
Healer, Book Four
Chaser, Book Five

Highlander's Castle

Highlander Heat, Book One

Joanne Wadsworth

Highlander's Castle
ISBN-13: 978-1-99-003414-5
Copyright © 2014, Joanne Wadsworth
Edited by Penny Barber
Cover Art by Joanne Wadsworth
First electronic publication: February 2014

Joanne Wadsworth
http://www.joannewadsworth.com

AUTHOR'S NOTE:
This book is a work of fiction. The names, characters, places, and incidents are products of the writer's imagination or have been used fictitiously and are not to be construed as real. Any resemblance to persons, living or dead, actual events, locale or organizations is entirely coincidental. The author does not have any control over and does not assume any responsibility for third-party websites or their content.

Published in the United States of America

First digital publication: February 2014
First print publication: September 2014

Dedication

To everyone who enjoys Highlander stories. I intend to keep these books coming.

Acknowledgements

Huge thanks go to my hubby, Jason, and kiddies, Marisa, Caleb, Cruise and Rocco, an incredibly supportive family who allow me so much time to write. My love for you is endless.

I also have the most amazing editor, Penny Barber. The absolute best.

For my readers, I can't thank you enough for joining me, and taking this journey to where imagination and magic soar.

Chapter 1

On the way to the ruins of Dunscaith Castle, on the Isle of Skye.

Anne MacLeod tapped her tour brochure against the front headrest as they traveled the bumpy road. Beyond the windshield, the ruins of Dunscaith Castle perched on a low headland to the side of the twisting and isolated road.

"Dunscaith Castle is one of at least four named as such, and in this remote area of Scotland, it took brute strength for clan MacDonald to hold it," her guide, Donald MacDonald, declared as he negotiated his way up the van's cramped aisle toward the front.

"Donald, it says here that sometime in the fourteenth century the MacLeods took control of it."

"They did, but the MacDonalds recaptured it again in the fifteenth century. There have been too many battles to count between my clan and yours here." A slow grin broke across his face. "Even during this entire trip, you and I have found plenty to bicker about."

"That's because you love to prattle on about your kin so much." MacDonalds. They were all impossible.

The heavy swell of the sea crashed into the cliff-face and sprayed the jagged ruins. Gray blocks of stone stood so heartbreakingly cold and alone, as she was on this tour. Goodness, how she'd have loved to have her parents by her side as she trekked through Scotland. They'd always longed to make the journey here, where centuries ago, their ancestors had lived. Even with all Donald's jabbering, these ruins intrigued her. MacLeods had lived here, and history had decreed her own kin had walked these moors.

"Donald, we're taking a look around, right?"

"Yes, we'll stop soon." He rubbed his jaw. "If you wish, you'll hear far more about your ancestors if you take the Dunvegan Castle tour. The MacLeods have ruled there for over eight-hundred years."

"Next week then. I'll make sure I book another tour with you since we get along so well."

He snorted a laugh. "You won't find me taking tours to Dunvegan. I leave that for one of their own. Come everyone. We're about to stop. It's blustery out so wrap up."

She hoisted to her feet, edged past Donald and tapped the kind elderly driver on the shoulder. "How safe are the ruins to walk around, William?"

"Not too bad. You'll have to mind the cliff's edge as you wander about since there's a gap of six meters or so between the mainland and the rock the castle sits on. The walled bridge arching between the two is unstable, and it's best to take the beach access. We'll be here for an hour. Do you have something warmer to put on over that blouse?" He wore thick corduroy trousers and a brown-speckled woolen jersey.

She patted her red ankle-length woven skirt, which she'd bought her first day after discovering how shockingly cold Scotland's weather could be. "I sure do. I can't wait to get out there and take a look around."

"I'll see to that now then." William indicated then jerked

over to the side of the road. "There's nothing like having one of your kin here to stir up some excitement. Keep Donald on his toes. My son needs the adventure."

"Dad, please. Don't beg trouble." Donald shoved open the side door and stepped out. The brisk breeze tossed his dark locks across his face as he fastened his coat. Her tour was run by a private family firm, and without her own family, she'd jumped at the chance to join Donald and William's.

"Thank you, William. Adventure is my middle name." She nabbed her red woolen coat from the back of her seat, hurried to the door and stepped onto the crumbly edged blacktop.

The salty scent of the sea tickled her nose. Fog clung to its choppy blue-green surface, a layer of it rolling in with the surging waves. The brisk Highland wind rushed at her, and she flicked up her collar. Scotland was so cold, nothing like New Zealand. At home she barely even wore a coat, yet here she'd likely need one all year round. How had her ancestors coped with living on this beautiful, yet ruggedly cold land?

"Where does your family hail from?" Buttoning his coat as he leaned against the side of the van, Donald eyed her. "You've quite the accent for a MacLeod."

"Didn't I tell you I'm from Down Under?"

"Australia?"

"No, a little further down than that."

"Antarctica?" Donald was such a tease. "Oh, you mean New Zealand?"

"Funny, and yes. You know, back home they have a name for someone like you?"

"What's that?"

"A pest."

He burst into laughter. "I'll get you back for that later."

"I'm sure you will. So how many family members have you got here? When I booked my ticket with your mother, she introduced me to three of your brothers, all taking different tours." This one was her first preference though. It would only be a short trek to the ruins along the rocky shore.

"Just those three, but I have what feels like a thousand cousins, and dozens of aunts and uncles." He motioned toward the stone rubble. "Go ahead if you'd like. I'll wait for the others and then follow."

"I think I will. Feel free to catch up. If you can." Grinning, she strode off. The shore track quickly reduced to a thin path through the long grasses and heather as it wound uphill to the mainland. At the top, she wiped her brow. A steep gully separated her and the ruins. The beach access must have been to the right of the decayed bridge, only fog rushing in obscured it. The bridge walls were intact. It might be possible to shuffle along the remaining narrow shelf. She leaned over the edge of the twenty-foot chasm then set one foot on the ledge.

Yep, her small feet would be a bonus. This was doable. Allowing her adventurous spirit to take flight, she stepped out. Even shrouded as it was, Dunscaith Castle awaited her.

"What are you doing, Anne? Wait." Donald jogged toward her. "You can't cross there. Dad told you to take the beach access to the side."

A gust plastered her long skirt against her legs. "Sorry, I'm a bit impulsive. I'll be fine."

"Get back."

"I'll be careful." She waved him off while maintaining her balance. Below the sea roared and the surf washed in to slap hard and spray high against the rock's sheer surface. Best to take it slow. She lowered and crawled.

"Wait up. Geez, we should never have let a MacLeod board the van." He braced one foot on the ledge.

"It's all right. I can make it on my own."

"I'm coming anyway. You're my responsibility."

"What about your other passengers?" A drop of water splashed her nose then another hit her cheek.

"They're taking the correct path since their hearing is better than yours."

"Then I'll see them at the ruins." Gosh, where was the end of the ledge?

"Got you." Donald clamped her ankle and held her still.

"Let go and stop ruining my fun. I'm almost there."

"Hold still or else you'll topple us both off."

"Don—" Lightning flashed and thunder boomed. A heavy cloud blackened the skies. "Right, holding still."

"Strange things have happened at these ruins over time, events that can't be explained."

"Can we back up? I can't see more than a few feet in front of—" A horse whinnied then the sound of hooves pounding echoed all around. "There's a horse out here?"

"No, not unless—"

Underneath her the ledge shook and through the shroud, a horse and rider rode free. Inches away on the wooden drawbridge, the animal reared up on its hind legs.

Shoot, that couldn't be right. Where had the drawbridge come from?

She clutched Donald as the horse's hooves crashed down, almost slicing into her.

"The castle belongs to us, Artair." A beast of a man riding the brute bellowed to another rider. "Dinnae let nary a MacLeod enter. I'll see to my mother and Anne."

"I'll return to the watch point." The man who must be Artair slapped his horse's rear and galloped back into the gloom.

"Alex." A Highlander wrapped in a thick plaid raced from the castle. "Where's the chief and the men he took with him?"

"We found no trace of him passing through the village." In one swift move, Alex dismounted then secured his destrier to a post on the bridge. "Cool the horse and give him an extra hand of oats, James." He stormed into the castle.

"Did you see that?" Anne fisted Donald's coat. "Who are

those men? What's going on?"

"This could be one of those strange things. I've heard it said—"

"Who goes there?" The Highlander, James, stomped forward in his thickly furred boots, hunkered down and looked right through her as if searching.

"I think he can hear us." She could certainly almost touch him, this warrior dressed as if from centuries in the past.

"Come forth and show yourself." The man shot out a hand, caught her around the neck and yanked her to her feet. "There you—Anne?" His bushy red eyebrows flung up. "Sorry, lass. I left you inside. How did you sneak past me?"

"Donald, help." She wobbled as he released her. Where was Donald? She fell to her knees and slapped the ledge where she'd just been. "Not funny, Donald. You can't desert me now. Show yourself."

"The chief's away. Alex returned, but couldnae find him." James heaved her up.

"Where on earth did this drawbridge come from?" She stomped on it. It was solid and very real. The planks were of the thickest cut. "Who are you?"

"The same man I was this morn. Come. Let's get you back inside."

"No, I have to find Donald and go home."

"This is your home. Now nay more wandering in the cold." He snatched her wrist and tugged her away.

"This is all a mistake." She heaved, but his grip was immoveable.

He steered her under an arch and along a stepped passageway with crenelated stone walls. They came out of the dank walkway and crossed an inner courtyard holding a central well. Stone buildings rose all around, although barely visible in the growing dark. He urged her up a side staircase.

"Please, you've got to stop."

"Once I deliver you to my brother. Alex," he bellowed. "I have your betrothed."

Betrothed? Holy moly, she wasn't betrothed to anyone. Why would this man think she was? "No. You have me confused with someone else. I shouldn't even be here, and I'm definitely not—"

"Anne, there you are." A woman dashed down the passageway. She wore a gown of rich burgundy with lace edging her bodice. "We still need to hem one of my gowns for your handfast. Good grief, I cannae believe 'tis been a sennight and your trunks have still no' arrived."

"My trunks? What do you mean by a sennight?"

"'Twill be all right. One of my gowns will suffice." Her accent was much thicker than Donald's. She rubbed Anne's woolen-coated arm. "Where did you get this garment? 'Tis of a bonnie weave, as is your skirt, but no' attire I've given you."

"I, ah…"

"Nay, never mind. The seamstress must have left it for you. The weaver woman has a new loom, and what a fine thread it weaves." She looked at James and huffed. "Let the lass go. I never taught you to manhandle a woman so."

"She lost her way. I was simply making certain she didnae again." He tucked his hands behind his back.

"What was the MacLeod chief thinking, James? When a man sends his kin to another's household, she should arrive with more than the clothes on her back."

"I'd say naught since she also arrived without a guard. Where's Alex? His bride tried to take flight."

"Here." Thick blond hair swept over Alex's shoulders as he stormed around the corner. "And the MacLeod chief likely hoped I'd send her straight back to Dunvegan Castle."

"That's no' possible," James muttered. "No one denies our uncle what he wishes."

"Aye, this handfast was brokered by him, and I'll accept

what will be in order to end this feud between us and the MacLeods." He halted before the woman, grasped her hands. "Uncle didnae travel through the village, and I couldnae find any other trace of his passage."

"You'll widen your search?"

"At first light, Mother. We'll find him."

His mother appeared young, her long brown locks only holding a strand or two of gray. While Alex wore a great plaid secured over his chest with a silver pin and belted low at his waist with a leather girdle.

A missing chief. A castle no longer in ruins. And a betrothal. She pinched herself. Ouch. Yes, this was real. She'd traveled back through time. Nothing else made sense. Yet, how did they all know her? "Ah, Alex. I'm confused."

"There's nay need to be. Come. You shouldnae have been outside." He opened the wooden door off the corridor. "You're shivering and should warm yourself. Your chamber awaits."

"Go stand afore the fire, my dear." The woman patted her shoulder then eyed Alex. "When will the ceremony take place?"

"On the morrow. Noon. Anne, if you will. We should speak since there has no' been time since your arrival."

Right, because for some reason they believed she'd already been here a week. She glanced from him to the chamber. Her choices seemed fairly limited. She needed to find out what was going on and more about this Anne they'd called her.

"Dinnae dally. Inside. 'Tis your chamber." James nudged her forward.

"I'm not a prisoner am I?" Best to check.

"Nay, no' once your vows are spoken. You'll be kin then."

Kin. She had no kin, and hadn't for three years. Still, she couldn't find out more unless she and Alex spoke. She entered and her intended shut the door. A large bed covered in blankets, the topmost cover a pretty patchwork of red and blue wool, sat against one wall. Under the window, a side table held a basin and jug, and next to it, a trunk sat propped open. She edged toward it. The engraving along its sides appeared Celtic in design, although nothing was contained within. No clothes, as said.

"Has Mary shown you around while I've been gone?"

"Ah, Mary's your mother." She tried not to make it a question. If she'd traveled to the past as it appeared, it'd be best to watch her words.

"Last I was aware." He smiled then quickly straightened his lips. "I apologize for the length of time I've been gone. We've no' had the chance to get to know one another as we should've."

"You mean before our vows are spoken?" Because those sounded imminent.

"Aye. Why did James find you outside?" He closed the wooden shutters over the narrow window then lit a candle from the fire blazing in the hearth.

"Now that's a whole other story. I think I hit my head. It feels a little fuzzy. You don't mind telling me what year this is, do you?"

He snorted, almost extinguishing the candle before he set it into its place on the corner stand. "'Tis the year of our reckoning, one where you and I must live together as man and wife. Pray tell it can occur between a MacDonald and a MacLeod."

"So it's like what? The fourteenth? The fifteenth? The sixteenth century?"

"Lass, we should speak of our ceremony. I'd like your word you'll honor your vows as I will honor mine."

"How do you intend our handfast to work?"

With a quizzical look, he closed in on her. "Your accent is more that of the Lowlanders, and you speak odd words. Were you no' raised with your cousin, the Chief of MacLeod?"

"I've been around a bit, which adds a flare to my accent." She'd have to take care and watch her words. And she was now cousin to the MacLeod chief? Strange didn't even begin to cover this.

"Clearly, and without a guard. You've abided within my walls with none of your own clansmen about, and aye, ours willnae be a typical handfast. I've no intention of"—he clasped his hands behind his back—"getting too close."

At least Alex seemed honorable. "Thank you. That'll be one less thing for me to worry about, and trust me, I currently have a few issues."

"Neither of us wished for what's befallen us. We'll cope as we must for the next year and a day."

"Will this handfast truly end the feud between our clans?" She'd heard of such things when she'd studied Scotland's history. A handfast wasn't as binding as a marriage and could easily be undone. It would probably suit a ton of people in her time.

"'Twill end the feud for longer should we make the effort." He crossed the room and stood before her.

"Could you expand on this effort?" She glanced at the bed. "I thought you just said—"

"I did." He cupped her cheek, brought her gaze back to his. "I meant it when I said we willnae be getting too close, but we still have to live with each other."

She stared into his eyes. Specks of gold flickered brightly within the brown. "You have the most beautiful eyes."

"I think no'."

"Your lashes are so long with sweeping golden tips." It wasn't like her to notice such a thing about a man. Yet it was as if a fairy had waved her wand and sprinkled a magical color over them.

"Anne." He shut his eyes then opened them.

"There's something about—" She covered his hand. Oh, so warm. She curled her fingers between his. Deep inside, something about him niggled with familiarity. "I must be hallucinating. It's as if we've met before, but that's entirely impossible."

"We have." He frowned. "You seem rather confused. Mayhap you need a rest after your wandering this eve."

"Yes, rest, and some time to myself." Great. Time. She was currently a few centuries out of that, but a little more wouldn't matter.

"Is there aught you need afore I say goodnight?" He turned his hand until their palms lay flush together.

That niggle exploded and she itched to get closer still. "No, I'm good." She rubbed her hand against his, his toughened skin rough yet so soothing. Her worry eased. She was in the past, but he was here. All would be well. This was more than strange.

"Then I'll see you in the morn. Goodnight, Anne. Sleep well." He pressed a kiss to the inside of her palm, stepped away with a curt bow and strode to the door.

Before she could call him back, he shut it with a resounding thunk.

Gone. Her heart squeezed tight. "Alex, you promised you'd never leave me." Her whispered words made no sense, and the honesty ringing within them made her shiver.

"Anne MacLeod?" A young woman rolled out from underneath the bed then slapped the dust from her long navy skirts as she stood.

She jumped back and clutched her chest. "Good grief. Where did you come from?"

"Under the bed." The woman smiled apologetically. "Sorry, 'tis no' the time to jest. My name's Anne MacLeod too, but my closest call me Annie. I didnae mean to frighten you."

"You're too late for that." Unbelievable. This woman had long hair, a shimmery shade of white-gold that swayed to her waist. She had the same shade and length, only her hair was wound up into a bun for the day. "Please tell me I'm hallucinating. Why do we look...identical?"

"You're one of my direct descendants." The woman edged closer. "Our lives are now tied together."

"How? Why?"

"I'll explain what I can. There's fairy blood within the MacLeod line, and on the last full moon, I made a wish upon the Fairy Flag hidden within Dunvegan Castle. I asked to travel to a place where I wouldnae be forced to handfast with the MacDonald. My wish took me through a portal from my time, and I witnessed the wonders of the twenty-first century right here on the Isle of Skye. Machines flew high above, boats motored across the water at great speed, and cars raced overland on a surface of black tar. I tasted sweets I never imagined could exist." She grinned and clasped Anne's hands. "The moving pictures of your television delighted me, and music one can plug into one's ears. Such miracles."

"You've been to my time." This was all real, very real.

"Aye, but only for a few days afore I was pulled back a sennight past."

"So, the Anne they think I am is clearly you. But why am I here?"

"'Tis my fault." She squeezed her hands. "My wish both took and gave. From my time it gave me the ability to travel forward, but for my wish to come full circle, it took the blood of my blood, and brought you to the past."

"How do you know all that?"

"The Fairy Flag is the most treasured possession of our clan, and 'tis hard no' to believe since I've seen what I now have."

"So I'm stuck here? For how long?"

"I dinnae know. I reactivated the portal at Dunvegan because I visited there in your time. Had I no', I may have remained in the future much longer. How did you arrive?"

"A thick fog descended as I toured these ruins then before I knew it, James pulled me through the portal. Why don't you want to handfast with Alex?"

"'Tis a long story. Yet I couldnae defy my cousin and go against his decision. Since my parents passed, he has cared for me. If it were no' me, then it would have been Margaret, Rory's sister, who would have had to come. She's too young, and my duty is to my clan. Anne, I dinnae know what will happen now. Do you have any kin who'll miss you?"

"No, my parents passed away three years ago. They died when our house caught fire, an electrical fault."

"Then I need to fix what I've started. Let me—" Form wavering, she clutched her belly. "Nay, something's happening."

"Annie, don't go." She grabbed her, but caught thin air as the woman disappeared. "Crap, that did not just happen." This had to be a really bad dream.

Except it wasn't, and the physical proof lay spread out before her. She was in Scotland, somewhere far in the past and about to handfast with a Highland warrior who had stirred something deep inside her. She should be petrified, and she was, but an equal sense of homecoming washed over her.

For some reason, or for every reason, she was meant to be here.

* * * *

Alone in the misty moonlight, Alex paced the barmkin. His bride had arrived on a foggy night like this one a sennight past. She'd insisted she'd been left on the mainland to make her final journey to Dunscaith alone, but why would MacLeod leave her beyond the gates then slink away into the dark? Surely he'd wish to witness their vows, to ensure they were honored.

The fact he hadn't, had roused both his and Uncle's suspicions. Donald had taken two of their guardsmen and set out to survey their lands, to find some sign of MacLeod's journey since Anne had surely not arrived by sea. Now Uncle had vanished. None in the village had seen him pass through, so where was he?

Footsteps echoed through the foggy haze and he swung around.

James appeared out of the mist. "There ye are. I've set a

guard near your bride's door in case she decides to make her way outside again."

"She willnae escape. Neither of us have a choice with the path we now take."

"Aye, and equally 'twill no' be a hardship by the looks of her. Her disposition is sweet too." James rubbed his stubbly jaw. "Mother has enjoyed her company."

"Mother wants to see the feud come to an end." When he and Donald had traveled to Dunvegan and signed an agreement for the coming handfast, Mother had applauded it.

"As we all do. 'Twas strange when I found her." James cleared his throat. "She appeared lost. She even called for Donald, as if our uncle would come to her rescue."

"You must have misheard her."

"Nay, I dinnae believe so."

Alex tapped James's ears. His brother, five years his junior at three and twenty, was a man he wouldn't be able to tease for much longer, but he still took every opportunity he could. "Aye, these lie too flat to your head."

"And yours flap too far and wide." Eager to topple him, James swept out his leg, except Alex countered the move, caught his brother's foot and tumbled him onto the hard ground. "Och, take care, I dinnae need bruises sprouting on your coming wedding day."

"My bride will no' be seeing your big rump."

"Flat ears and a big rump? I think we need to have a wee sparring match with the blade." James pushed to his feet and dusted off his hands. "Will dawn—"

The horn sounded with one long and eerie blast across the bay. Alex jumped to attention. "That'll be Artair. I'll take Fergus and see what he needs. Maintain a tight guard on watch."

Something was afoot and with Uncle away, Dunscaith was his responsibility.

He wouldn't fail him.

Chapter 2

A chilling horn shrilled through the whistling wind. Anne flung the shutters open and wedged sideways out the window. Horses' hooves pounded across the earth through the sludge of fog then faded as the horses galloped away.

"Anne, it's me." Mary hurried into her room. "Oh, it's cold in here. Let me close the window." She bustled past, drew the shutters back then gripped Anne's hands. "Why did James find you outside? Were you truly trying to escape?"

"No, I was—"Any talk of what had actually happened would be considered the ramblings of an insane person, or even a witch considering she was in the past. Right now, she couldn't put any of these people offside, which meant she shouldn't speak of Annie and her conversation with her ancestor. "I was curious. I love the outdoors. That's all."

"Then wait until once you're wed afore you explore. I'll show you farther afield. How was your conversation with Alex? Do you feel more relaxed? He would never harm you, no' when we need this feud to end."

"I don't fear him. Your son is…" Well he was a strapping warrior and a rather appealing one at that.

"Mayhap you fear your wedding night then?" Mary drew

her toward the bed and urged her to sit. "Since your parents passed and your mother would have had this conversation with you, if you need, I could speak of what will occur."

In truth, she wasn't experienced. Her parents had died after her eighteenth, and not one relationship she'd had since had jelled enough for her to take that next step. "Ah, sure, go ahead."

"There will be some discomfort." Mary's cheeks flushed. "I was wed a month shy of my sixteenth, and Alex arrived within the first year."

"Is there just him and James?"

"Oh nay. Alex is the eldest, and James the youngest, but I have a daughter between. She will come home and bring her family with her for the Twelfth Night and Yule celebrations." She clasped her hands in her lap. "Ask what you will."

"I barely know Alex, and I'd rather..." Oh, how did she put this?

"You dinnae wish bairns yet?"

In this age, a woman who didn't want children might seem treacherous. Plus she was protected. Best to play the part of a woman truly from this time, and really, sharing a bed with Alex did appeal. His golden eyes had been far too delicious.

"Anne?"

"Sorry. I'd like bairns, but with a handfast is it wise?"

"I've always wished for Alex to have a wife and kin. Should you get with child, Alex would wed you proper. I know my son." She whispered, "The day I learnt of the agreement Alex had signed, I was terribly relieved. No matter the means which has brought you here, to me you will be my daughter." Mary's eyes blazed with her heartfelt declaration.

"I don't know what to say."

"Our lives are dictated by our men, although we hold sway where we can. I shall teach you all you need to know."

Her chest lightened. "This place is all so new to me. I'll do my best to get to know Alex."

"Good." Mary squeezed her arm. "'Twill be a long day on the morrow, so get some rest. I'll bring a suitable gown for your ceremony then."

"Thank you. Your kindness means—" She blinked back tears, overwhelmed by how intensely her emotions had risen. "I don't feel so alone anymore."

She'd hated how alone she'd been. With no grandparents, siblings, aunts or uncles, it had been just her for so long. Traveling to Scotland had been her way of searching for a link to family, no matter how remote.

"Even surrounded by so many of your own clansmen, my dear?"

Right, Annie must have plenty of other family. "Even so."

"I understand. Nevertheless, we must forge our place where we can, and do what we must." She rose and swished to the door. "Rest well, and no more attempts of escape."

"Yes, goodnight." She must be here for a reason, even if one currently beyond her comprehension.

* * * *

Alex rode hard down the trail toward the watch point Artair guarded. 'Twas hard to believe no sign had been found of Uncle.

Fergus galloped beside him, as did two other men. "What's your plan, Alex?" Fergus shouted.

"Artair and I returned from the village. The chief was no' seen passing through and neither was clan MacLeod."

Anne had arrived alone, but she'd insisted she'd had an escort to the fringes of MacDonald land. He should have spoken to her about it tonight after his return, except with her escape it had slipped his mind. Later. He would raise the issue with her and demand an answer.

"The MacLeods could've taken the sea-route," Fergus offered.

"Since they never came ashore at Dunscaith, they would have had to make berth at the village then hire horses to complete the journey here. They still would have been sighted had they arrived by that path."

"So where's our chief?"

He had no idea, couldn't even fathom why he'd not yet returned. Although, Uncle was alive. He had to be. Eying Fergus, he grit out, "At first light, I want you to search farther than the village. Anne couldnae have traveled to Dunscaith alone. She would never have survived the trip."

Outlaws would certainly consider the sight of a young woman traveling the forests alone fair game. He tightened his grip on his reins. No harm could befall his intended. Not only would the Chief of MacLeod see it as a means to reinstate their fight, but now he'd talked with Anne, he wouldn't wish to see her harmed. She was an innocent, and once they spoke their vows, she was his to care for. He wouldn't fail in that duty.

They rode on until they passed a guard stationed at the perimeter of the trail. He slowed his mount, his men following suit.

From behind the bushes, Artair slid out and hailed him over. "Alex, our tartan has been found by one of the men searching along the shore. 'Twas unexpected with it being so far from the village route." He pulled a scrap of plaid from under his girdle and handed it across.

After fingering the weave, Alex brought it to his nose. 'Twas clear of any scent except that of the sea. "'Tis certainly a marker."

"Aye, but why would the chief veer so far off the path? The guard stationed here at the time said he'd gone by way of the forest."

"Then he must have changed his mind." Alex tossed Fergus the cloth. "You've a new direction. If there is one marker, there will be others. Follow them until you find our chief or hear word of where he's traveled."

"I willnae rest until he's found."

"Good, neither will I." He nodded to Fergus and Artair, turned his horse and rode back to the keep. He would have a word with his bride-to-be tonight. They did not need mistrust between them.

As he galloped toward the drawbridge, the mist rose like a ghostly veil waiting to be swept away by the coming dawn. He called out his arrival, and a lad raced to take his stead. Inside, he stormed up the tower and dispatched the guard from outside Anne's chamber. 'Twas time.

He strode in then halted. The room held a cold bite, and Anne slept curled up within her blankets. Damn. Best to see to her comfort first. He rebuilt the fire until it blazed.

"Mmm." Anne rolled over.

He dusted his hands as he stood. Her sweet rose scent drew him closer toward her. So seductive. A wild copse of white roses grew along the entrance of the forest path and it held the same perfume, a fragrance bidding riders both welcome and farewell.

"Mum, Dad, I'll find..."

During the contract signing, he'd learnt she'd lost her parents. Such an innocent, her face softly curved, her nose tiny, and high cheeks sprinkled with freckles. She stretched one arm over her head and wriggled as if enjoying the toasty warmth spreading through the room.

"Mmm, Alex." She pushed her other arm out, dislodging her blankets.

Hell. She wore no nightrail, and her full breasts, barely covered, pushed toward him.

Eyes closed, she continued to murmur, "You promised to never leave me."

Lust shot straight to his cock. He itched to slide the last inch of her bedding away, to caress her firm roundness. This image of her would surely haunt him.

Damn, he shouldn't have said they wouldn't be getting too close. A handfast gave him all the rights of a marriage but with the ease of repudiation. He could bed her if he wished. No one would gainsay him.

He stomped to the chair before the window, sat and kicked his feet onto the trunk. He couldn't wake her, and he should have sought his bed, except Anne's gentle breathing lulled him to sleep.

* * * *

The soft rays of dawn that pierced the horizon stirred him from his slumber. A silvery-pink hue glittered over the loch's still waters. The night had gone and his wedding day reared. His bride. She lay so temptingly close.

Her eyelids fluttered open and she pushed herself upright, allowing those atrocious blankets to slither into her lap and expose her breasts.

"Alex? Is that you?" She rubbed her eyes.

"Aye." He averted his gaze. "My apologies. I didnae mean to—"

She gasped and the blankets rustled. "Sorry about that. I'm decent now. I heard a horn last night then horses riding out. Is everything okay?"

He coughed into his fist then brought his gaze back to hers. "A marker was found last eve, one the chief left behind."

"You've found him then?"

"Nay, but one of my men will go in search of him this morn."

"You didn't want to go?"

"We have vows to speak."

"Of course." She shuffled to the side of the bed, pulled a bundle of clothing off the side table then dove under the blankets with them. Hidden, she dressed. "Although I understand if you must go. He's your uncle."

Did she wish to delay their handfast? Or mayhap she was truly offering him this kind consideration. As yet he didn't know her well enough to guess. "You will speak your vows, as I will.

They come first."

"That's not what I meant." She emerged from under the covers, shoved her tangled white-blond tresses from her face and met his gaze. "I actually don't have an issue with us getting hitch—I mean, handfasted. It's not like it's permanent."

"You truly dinnae mind?" When he'd first arrived at Dunvegan, MacLeod had requested her presence. Anne hadn't shown herself, and eager to leave, he'd set sail.

"Your mother's so nice. I can handle whatever time I'll have here." She eased her feet to the floor and stood. "I fear we've gotten off to a bad start, but I'm here now, and I'm going to make the best of it. So, where do we stand?"

Her words made little sense. Where they stood was perfectly clear. Arms crossed, he strode to her. "Any lies between us are unacceptable. There has never been a sign MacLeod brought you. How did you arrive without an escort, my lady?"

"You think I traveled alone? Without guardsmen?"

"Nay, but there's no other answer than that."

She skimmed his forearms then dipped her fingers into the gap where they crossed. "If I told you the truth, you'd have me locked away."

"I would still have the truth over any lie. I willnae abide my own wife withholding."

"I barely know you." She smiled. "Although I gather I soon will."

"I would never hurt you. You need only speak the truth." He couldn't help tracing a finger over her full lower lip. Her beautiful smile caused her dimples to show. "How did you arrive?"

"Just promise me you won't lock me up if I answer you." She licked her lips and as she did, her tongue swept over the tip of his finger.

He wanted to capture that tongue and taste her for himself.

He cleared his suddenly dry throat. "Aye, you have my word."

"I didn't arrive by the usual means."

Mayhap she needed more encouragement. "The truth will set you free."

"Usually, but in my case, and in this time, I don't think so."

"As my wife, 'tis my duty to protect you." She was his, and his protection was absolute.

"I haven't been anyone's duty in a long time. I don't expect it from you, no matter the length of time I'm here. All I ask is that we might be friends."

She wished a friendship? With him? "You ask the impossible."

"Or possible." Blue eyes twinkling, she held out her hand as if expecting him to shake it as men did.

Instead he shook his head. His forthcoming bride had strange ways about her.

* * * *

"Please, I'll tell you the truth if we agree on a friendship first." A friendship was what Anne wanted, particularly with this man who would become her husband.

"You jest." He coughed, rather haggardly.

"No, and we've already covered the whole no lying thing. Alex, I could seriously use a friend so far from home. Mary is lovely, but we'll be wed, and honestly, wouldn't it be nicer to pass the time enjoying each other's company? You never know, you may even like me."

"There's nay need for it, but if you insist, I'll offer friendship for the truth." He caught her hand, brushed a kiss to her knuckles then released her. "How did you arrive at—"

A knock sounded on the door and Mary peeked in. "Oh, sorry to interrupt. Anne, I've ordered your bath, and the seamstress is waiting to see to your gown."

"Come in. Alex was saying hello."

"Oh, listen to you and your unusual words. Do you mean

good morn?"

"I did. I've picked up a few new expressions and terms on my journeys, and enjoy using them from time to time." An adequate explanation, hopefully.

"How wonderful. You must tell me of them when there's time. Good morn, Alex." Grinning, Mary played with the white ribbon threaded along the front of her emerald gown. "The fog has cleared, and 'twill be a beautiful day."

"You appear happy, Mother."

"Fergus informed me you'd found a marker. He left at first light with another of our best trackers."

"Aye. We'll find the chief, and soon."

"James has cleaned up rather well. You should take a dip in the loch too." Her eyes sparkled with mischief. "Your bride must have no idea of the fine features you hide under all that dust you've picked up in your travels."

He rubbed his heavily whiskered jaw. "As only a mother would say."

Anne laughed. It had been so long since she'd witnessed a family's closeness like this. Her parents had always shared a special bond, and had lavished attention on their only child. She'd missed this, family, teasing and togetherness. "He looks fine to me." She rubbed his bristles. "A little furry, but I can deal."

"You've picked up more than a few new expressions. I'll go bathe. We'll speak later." He dipped his head then stepped away. "Mother, make sure my bride isnae late."

"Midday. I have no' forgotten." He left and Mary chuckled. "My, my. What a nice surprise to find Alex taking the time to learn more about you."

"We've agreed to a friendship. It's a start."

"More than a start."

Another knock sounded and Mary opened the door. A seamstress scurried in, a white damask gown folded neatly over her arm.

"This is my wedding dress, Anne." Mary lifted the shimmery silk woven into a lacelike pattern.

"It's beautiful." The bodice was cut boldly low and trimmed with lace. So extravagant. "Are you certain you wish to lend it to me?"

"My family spoilt me, as I shall spoil you. Please wear my gown. My daughter did."

"I—I always wanted to wear Mum's dress when I married, only it was lost in a fire." It too had been made of white damask, only the fire that had taken it, had in turn taken her parents' lives too. She fought back the sudden threat of tears. She was stronger than this, but it was a momentous day, one her parents should never have missed.

"Then wear it, and think of your mother. She'll be watching from the heavens, I'm sure."

"Thank you." Mary knew what to say. "She would have liked you."

"Such a compliment. Thank you." She turned to the seamstress. "Let's get to work. I wish to see my new daughter wed in this gown."

The seamstress was a perfectionist, fitting and pinning the fabric to her. She took in every little nip. Once satisfied, she helped her step out of it then perched on the corner chair with it laid over her lap. From her basket, she selected needle and thread and set to work stitching.

At another knock, Mary crossed the room and bid a serving girl to enter. She placed a breakfast tray laden with a bowl of oats and honey on the side table. Two lads followed, heaving a wooden tub between them. They set it before the fire then hurried out as more servants arrived with pails of steaming water.

"Come. Time for you to eat." Mary pulled out a chair and patted it.

Yes. Her belly gurgled. It had been far too long since she'd last eaten. She swirled the honey over the oats and ate as Mary oversaw the tub filling. After the servants left, she discarded her clothes and bathed. So refreshing. She lazed with her head on the rim while Mary sang a gentle Scottish song of bens and burns, and of the hearth and home. Words that made little sense, yet she understood them all the same. "I love that tune. My mum often sang when she bustled about her kitchen. They remind me of the good times."

"I sang them to my bairns too, and I shall teach you the words if you'd like." Mary held out a drying cloth. "Though after you're wed. Alex willnae be happy if we're late."

She stepped out of the tub, wrapped the cloth around her and sat before the fire. Mary fussed over her. She brushed her hair until it gleamed then threaded dainty white silk flowers in a ribbon across the top.

The seamstress rose and smoothed the gown. "'Tis done, my ladies."

"Wonderful." Mary reverently examined the dress then grinned. "Perfect. Are you ready, Anne?"

"I better be." She stepped into the gown, and Mary quickly laced the stays. The lacy fabric flowed smoothly over her curves.

"You look stunning, my dear." Mary pinched her cheeks. "And 'tis noon. We must be away."

She twirled. "I feel like a princess."

"Mayhap a fairy, and since you're a MacLeod, 'tis in your blood."

Yes. The Fairy Flag at Dunvegan had been gifted decades ago by the fairy princess to the son she'd had with the MacLeod chief after falling in love with him. She'd wrapped their firstborn in the crimson and yellow patterned cloth as she'd sung him to sleep, a story told down through the generations. It was the Fairy Flag Annie had wished upon and the same flag she'd viewed from the future at Dunvegan, which had brought her back again to the past. That Fairy Flag had a lot to answer for. So did Annie. She'd love to know more about her. Where had she disappeared to? And what would she do to make this all right?

"What has that worried look on your face?" Mary straightened the long sleeves of lace so they sat lower on Anne's wrists.

"That I mustn't forget the Fairy Flag, nor Dunvegan. But for now, Alex is waiting."

"Aye, my son can be an impatient man. Let's go."

She followed Mary out the door. Theirs wasn't a real marriage, but a sense of rightness twitched within her heart. She wanted this.

The emotion expanded as she stepped outside. In the bright daylight, the courtyard, part thick with grass and part paved with stone, led to one place. Alex.

Her Highlander from another time stood beside a well adorned with ivy and lavender. The castle walls rose majestically around him.

Over an immaculate white silk shirt, he'd fastened his plaid with a magnificent hand-sized broach depicting warriors at war. Her warrior clasped the hilt of his side-belted sword.

His jaw was smooth and strongly angled, his chin holding a visible cleft, and his golden gaze was targeted right on her. Oh, what a shame this wasn't a marriage in truth. What a prize he'd make.

"Anne?" Mary patted her shoulder. "Alex awaits."

"Yes." Anticipation bubbled through her. Deep within her heart, she was more than ready, only why? What was it about Alex that drew her to him?

* * * *

Like an ethereal vision, Anne glided toward Alex. She reached him and he couldn't help fingering her waist length locks. Even the sun's rays feasted on her, setting her white-gold hair ablaze.

Damn. How would he keep his hands off her when she looked this edible? "You look…bonnie."

"Thank you." Her sapphire eyes burst with brightness. "You've washed up well yourself."

Edible and delightful. He was in a world of trouble. He turned to his brother. "Do you have our plaid?"

"Aye, here." James unraveled a strip of MacDonald tartan.

"Good." This was it. The moment he'd not wished for, but now strangely did. He clasped his right hand with Anne's right, and his left hand with her left then took a long, steadying breath. He looked into her eyes. She would be his wife, soon.

"It'll be all right." She squeezed his fingers. "This is meant to be. I wouldn't be here otherwise."

'Twas as if she spoke to his heart. "James will wrap the plaid around our hands and bind us together." He nodded at his brother and James tightened the strap around their joined hands. The symbolic gesture had his pulse racing. Nay, this was simply a handfast, which was real enough, but that's all. There would be no marriage in a year's time.

"Let's begin." He cleared his throat. "I, Alexander William MacDonald, nephew of the Chief of MacDonald, pledge my troth to Anne MacLeod. With this handfast, I take her as my wife for the next year and a day. Your turn." He tightened his grip on her hands.

"Well, that sounds easy enough." She edged closer, touching the silk tips of her slippers to his boots. "I, Anne MacLeod, cousin of...the Chief of MacLeod, pledge my troth to Alexander William MacDonald. With this handfast, I take him as my husband for the next year and a day, or until I no longer reside in his home."

"Nay, you will reside here. There can be no stipulation."

"Of course, that's what I meant."

James nudged his arm. "She resides here. Now hurry and kiss your bride. Seal the vows."

"Aye." He wanted to taste her lips this once, and he must seal the vows. "You ready, lass?"

"To a friendship like no other." She pressed her palms against his chest, and her touch seared his skin.

"Like no other." His heart pounded as he lowered his mouth to hers and kissed her soft lips. Damn. A spike of need rushed through him and he couldn't stop himself. He urged her lips apart and plunged deeper. Sweet heaven, she tasted delicious, and her escaping moan had him greedy for more.

"Alex." His brother slapped him on the back. "My good wishes to you and your bride. 'Tis time to feast. Mother and I will meet you inside the great hall."

The grin on Mother and James's faces as they strolled away had his frustration rising.

"Relax. It was just a kiss."

"We cannae allow that to happen again."

"If you say so." She shrugged and tried to wriggle one hand free of the binding. "Gosh, James sure knows how to tie a knot."

"Here, allow me." He jerked on the knot and instead tightened it further.

She giggled, her cheeks flushing pink. "I'll get this. I was a Girl Scout in my younger days and a whiz at the knot-tying badge."

"What's a Girl Scout?" She truly must have journeyed afar.

"It's a girl who goes scouting and must perform certain tasks before being awarded a badge." She examined the knot then used her teeth to tug at the lower loop. "I'm guessing I'm the first Girl Scout you've met?"

"Girls dinnae need to scout. We have warriors for that."

"I see. What may girls do in this—ah, now?" After working one loop loose, she moved to the next.

"Needlepoint, perhaps a musical instrument." Her warm breath caressed the inside of his wrist and sent desire shooting through him.

"Almost got it," she mumbled as she nibbled. "And I'm not good with anything musical. I'm more of an outdoors kind of girl."

"Nay, MacLeod permitted you to participate in outdoor activities?" What kind of chief allowed such a thing?

"Yes, swimming is a favorite. I bet I could beat your fastest warrior in the loch."

"I'm the fastest, and nay, 'tis impossible." He'd never permit her to swim with his men.

"You say that a lot. Wanna bet I can?" She wriggled another loop loose then slyly eyed him. "Say yes. My father, when he lived, loved to bet with me. He used to say it encourages one's drive to succeed."

"The loch is too cold for you at this time of the year." He wouldn't back down.

"With how fast I swim, I'll not even feel the chill. Are you worried I might win?"

"Nay, are you done with the knot?"

She rubbed her cheek to the back of his hand as she gave the last loop a tug. The tartan stretched enough for her to slide one hand free. "Got it. See, being a Girl Scout came in handy today."

"Thank you." He unraveled the remainder of the binding. "Come, allow me to feed my Girl Scout." He guided her inside, led her to the dais at the front of the great hall. With the chief away, he took the prime spot and offered her the seat on his left.

"I was certain that knot would hold you two together for much longer." James winked at him.

"Aye, but apparently I've wed a Girl Scout."

Before him, his clansmen filled their trenchers with thick slabs of meat and roasted vegetables. Serving girls weaved in and out, filling tankards with ale.

He loaded his own trencher, set it between him and Anne then offered her first choice. She ate, and once certain she was content, he turned toward James. "I want you to take a personal message to Rory MacLeod. Inform him the handfast vows have been spoken, that our agreement's been fulfilled and he should have been here to witness them himself."

"Consider it done." James nodded. "I'll take some of the men with me. They'll relish the trip."

"Do that." Good. His duty to his clan was done, although his one to Anne had just begun. He had a wife, and one far more tempting than he'd like. He wrapped an arm around her waist and drew her closer to his side.

"Are you all right?" She gazed into his eyes.

"I'm simply ensuring your comfort." Like hell he was. He still couldn't keep his hands off her.

She smiled and her happiness dazzled him.

What had he gotten himself into?

He'd wed a woman he could never be friends with.

Chapter 3

Beautiful tapestries, of hunting and landscape scenes, hung every ten feet around the great hall, except for over the fireplace where a massive claymore, its silver and gold hilt encrusted with rubies and emeralds took pride of place. The sword appeared far too big for any one man to hold, let alone swing in battle. Anne turned toward Mary seated next to her. "Is that real?"

"Aye, 'tis a beauty. Alex wields it."

She picked up her silver goblet and stroked the fine engraving. Everything brought delight to her eye, even the MacDonald clan. They'd grown in revelry as the afternoon had worn on, and now as evening descended the music flowed. Many danced, kicking up their heels to the lively piper tunes.

Tapping her feet under the table, she selected a morsel of salmon from the trencher she shared with Alex. She slipped it between her lips then savored the delectable flavor. So fresh. The sugared plums appeared sweetly ripe. She popped one into her mouth and moaned. Delicious. Highlanders certainly knew how to feast.

"Good tidings, Alex." Yet another clansman approached her new husband and offered a nod to her.

"How are your wife and son?" Alex responded. He'd spent

most of the day chatting with others and whenever they'd been a lull in the queue, James had taken his attention.

"Anne, do you like the pipers?" Mary jiggled in her chair as if eager to join those dancing.

"They're magnificent, and the girl who's singing is a delight."

"My lady." One of the clansmen addressed Mary. "Would ye care for a birl?"

"Oh aye." She bounded to her feet. The hulking man spun her away.

Now, that's what she wanted. She slid her hand around Alex's arm and his gaze jolted to hers. "It's a beautiful evening for a dance."

His jaw went slack. "I dinnae partake in such activities."

"It's easy. You move one leg and then the other. All you have to do is keep a rhythm going."

"I still prefer no' to—"

"Superb." She hauled him up.

"Nay, Anne."

"Really, you just need to move a little." She wrapped her arms around his neck. "I promise it won't hurt."

"I dinnae dance." He gripped her hips and tried to urge her back down.

"No, you don't." She rested her cheek on his chest. "I'll ease you into it slowly. Every girl should get to dance on her handfast day."

"No one dances like this."

"People actually do. You simply haven't seen it yet. I did mention my travels." She'd loosen him up.

He growled then muttered, "Here, at least let's do this where we can't be seen."

Ahh, success. Her Highlander had a soft streak no matter how big and tough he looked.

"I cannae believe I'm giving in to you." He ushered her into a hidden alcove behind the dais.

"Don't think of it as giving in, but instead coming on board. It's a great way to start our relationship." She snuggled against him. "We'll even call this our first dance."

"A relationship?" He swayed ever so slightly to the playful tune.

"Mmm-hmmm. Don't you think our handfast warrants being called one?" She certainly did, although what a shame to have agreed simply to a friendship. Oh, the things he likely knew and could teach her. Hold on. Any relationship she embarked on with him wouldn't have any lasting consequences. She had protection. And until Annie had fixed what she'd done, she may as well enjoy herself.

"More so by the second, lass." He slid a finger under her chin, lifted her gaze to his. "This handfast was forced upon us, but that does no' mean we cannae benefit from it in some way. If both parties were willing."

"Tell me what you mean, exactly."

"I'll make it abundantly clear." He leaned into her until her shoulders grazed the paneled walls behind. "Since we spoke this morn, I've become aware of you in ways beyond friendship. If you wish a relationship then I wish one too." His husky voice held dark, sensual promise.

"You truly mean that?" *Please, please, mean that.* "Because I could easily be swayed to your way of thinking."

"Aye, and 'tis you who has the most beautiful eyes." He pressed his hands flat against the wall either side of her, dipped his head and completed the trap. "I want the right to sleep in your bed, or I should say, to keep you in mine."

Oh, yes, yes, yes. "I've waited a long time to be with a man, so I have one stipulation. I won't accept you sleeping with anyone else while we're together. Can you accept that?"

"If you wish." He pressed his body against hers and she tingled everywhere they touched. "I must kiss you."

He covered her mouth with his, his lips so achingly soft. Oh, the taste of him swarmed her senses. She wanted more. He licked her tongue and his desire had her arching against him. She couldn't fight this attraction, didn't even have a hope of doing so. "Okay. Your bed. Now. We have a new deal."

He swept her into his arms and bounded up the stairs to his chamber. Carefully, he set her on the end of his enormous four-poster bed dominating the room. "Are you sure, Anne?"

"At the speed you ran, I better be." She stroked the thick fur pelt underneath her.

"I am." He removed her slippers then tugged her up and turned her around. He unlaced her stays, his warm breath feathering across each inch of skin he exposed.

"You seem rather experienced with dresses, not that I'm complaining." She clutched the front so it didn't slip.

"I've wished to remove this one since the moment I saw you in it."

"Well take your time. I haven't done this before." Great, now was not the time to get nervous.

"I'll take immense care." He spread his hands over her hips. "Turn around."

Her heartbeat raced. She was ready for this. Beyond ready. She turned.

* * * *

Anne faced him, and Alex took one of her hands in his. She still clutched the fabric over her breasts. "You have naught to worry about. I'll never hurt you. Pass me your other hand."

"It's not worry. I'm not sure how to explain this, but it feels like I've been waiting a lifetime for this moment. That makes no sense, but neither does me being here."

"You're here because you're mine." No matter the agreement in place, she was his.

"Yes, yours." She let go and her dress slithered down and clung perilously to her hips.

"I want to touch you. May I?"

"Stop asking and start doing."

He cupped her breasts, their fullness almost spilling out of his hands. Groaning, he thumbed her peaking nipples. "This morn I ached for what you now offer."

She lifted onto her toes and with the lightest of caresses, touched her lips to his. "Then take and don't hold back. I've been alone for too long. No more."

His cock pushed toward her as if trying to spear through his plaid. He had to have her now. He licked her nipple. Hell, she tasted divine, like the sweetest nectar, and naught could halt him from sucking her harder.

She shivered and arched fully into him. He feasted on her, but it wasn't enough. He gorged on her other breast.

"Oh my." Her breath whooshed out. "That feels incredible."

"This dress must go." He flicked the last lacing and it fell in a heap to the floor. She stood bared to his gaze, the fire's dancing flames casting a golden glow over her pale skin.

Every contour of creamy skin called to him, and between her thighs, white-gold curls shimmered. "You're so beautiful, Anne. I cannae believe you're mine."

"And you, Alex, are overdressed." She unhooked the broach over his chest and unraveled his plaid. "Take your shirt off so I can see exactly what you've promised is mine in return."

"Yes, my lady." He hauled the last obstruction over his head and her gaze dropped to his cock.

"Can I touch?" She licked her lips, and her clear desire hardened him further.

"Later. I need to get my fill of you first." He scooped her up and laid her on his bed. Her hair floated over his pillow and he nuzzled into the silky length and breathed deep. "Your scent is intoxicating."

She smiled and clasped his face. "You have a way with words."

"They are only for you." Allowing his passion its release, he kissed her. He would claim his bride, and she would be his in every way.

"I love the way you kiss." She rubbed her chest against his, her hard nipples grazing his flesh. "Show me everything. I never want to forget this night."

He kissed her, allowing his hunger to reign.

Aye, he'd show her everything.

They would never know such fulfillment as they did this eve.

* * * *

Anne couldn't halt her hips from pushing against Alex's. He'd awakened her body. Amazing. Wishes truly could come true.

She clutched her Highlander's broad shoulders then caressed his roped biceps. Big and strong. Wanting to touch all of him, she skimmed down his arms and over his hands. Her warrior from another time was built to battle and conquer, and right now, he was doing a fine job with her. He sucked her nipples, both soothing the need deep within and inflaming an equal need for more. Surrounding her, hot and hard, he intensified that heat.

"I need to touch more of you." He stroked her sides, cupped her bottom and brought her tight into him. "Rub against me."

"You want friction?" She massaged him with her body. "Like this?"

"Aye, your body fits mine."

"Or yours fits mine."

"I've never known such temptation as you." He dipped his fingers between them and glided along the inside of her thigh.

"Neither have I." Craving a deeper touch, she eased her legs apart. Her mind raced in a hundred different directions but they all led to one place. "Don't stop."

"I willnae." He swept his hand over her entrance, his

intimate touch scalding her. Then he plunged one finger inside. "I'll make this good for you."

He stroked deep inside then curled one finger into a spot that had her almost catapulting off the bed and would have if he hadn't held her down.

Oh, Alex was about to teach her more than she'd ever dreamed. This would certainly be a night she'd never forget.

* * * *

Hands on her hips, Alex slowly, carefully, moved between Anne's legs and nudged his cock along her slick folds. "Open wider for me, my sweet."

She spread her legs further. "I know there'll be a little pain."

"Only a pinch, and then it'll be gone."

"I trust you."

Her words undid him.

Covering her mouth with his, he demanded a response, which would distract her mind. Then he pushed against the barrier, tore through and plunged deep inside.

Her gasp was muffled against his neck as she held on piercingly tight.

"'Tis done." He stared into the depths of her restless gaze. "We're one."

"I like the way you said that. What are you waiting for?" She clutched his butt and urged him on. "Give me everything you promised."

"I'll give you your heart's desire." With one hand on her hip, he eased up slowly then gently pushed back in. She moaned, and he increased his pace until his thoughts were consumed by her. He pounded, hard and deep, taking her frantically as she encouraged him.

"So good." She raked her fingers down his back then screamed his name.

He was lost as her inner muscles tightened and dragged him in. Filling her completely, he spilled his seed deep, his release violent as he exploded along with her.

"Lovers," he whispered as he slumped on top of her, spent. "For as long as I can keep you."

* * * *

The wave of pleasure sweeping through Anne slowly receded. Alex lay heavily on top of her, but it was wondrous having him this close. She didn't want him to move, and she certainly hadn't expected how incredible her first time would be. She caressed the corded muscles of his damp back.

Wow, talk about a man of action. He was a warrior who could slay, and in more places than one. How was he all hers?

"Anne." His breath tickled her ear. "Are you sore?"

"No, I'm blissfully content. What about you?"

He rocked his hips and his shaft stirred and lengthened inside her. "'Tis been a while for me, but you can be assured I'm equally so."

"You want to teach me something else new?" Surely he wouldn't say no. "Because I promise I'm up for the lesson."

He chuckled then rocked faster. "What wonders do you wish now?"

"We've already agreed on it being everything." She sighed as he continued to rise and fill her. "I've missed you, Alex."

"I'm right here, lass."

"I know." They were finally one, as they always should have been.

"I dinnae intend to relinquish you. Are you ready for everything?"

His words sent a thrill through her, and his kiss took her places she more than desired. Below he stroked deep, as if touching the very heart of her. Her new handfast husband didn't know it yet, but he'd opened a new world of sensation she had no intention of giving up. She wanted more, and as much as could give her in whatever time they had.

He increased his rhythm then rubbed her clit. Oh, sooo

good. She moved with him, giving him more of the friction he'd asked for before.

"Come when you wish." He pushed his long length in then drew out, his kisses matching the same ebb and flow as below.

Her orgasm built. "I want this to last forever."

"Nay, I need to hear you scream my name." He grinned, and with one decisive flick of his finger over her clit, he made her come, so staggeringly fast.

Crying out his name as he'd wished, she convulsed around him. She rode the waves then crashed hard as he suddenly stiffened and jerked out. He groaned as if in pain before spilling himself on the bedding.

"Are you all right?" She rolled toward him. "Alex?"

"Aye. I cannae risk getting you with child." He seized her hand and held it firm over the heavy beat of his heart. "The first time I couldnae stop, but I must no' come inside you again."

"What? Seriously? I don't believe that actually works."

"It does. I've yet to father a bairn."

He couldn't father one with her anyway. Should she tell him?

Yes. She didn't want any lies between them. She wanted the trust she'd already placed in him to grow.

"Alex, whether you do that or not, I won't get with child. I'm safe for a couple of years."

"Impossible."

"It's true." Argh, what would it hurt if she told him she was from the future? They were wed, and she'd already given him her body. He deserved to know the truth. "You asked me how I arrived here alone and unescorted. What if I said, I came from the future? A time centuries from now and a place filled with wonders beyond your imagination. Women can actually take contraceptives for protection. That's what I've done."

He groaned. "Again, impossible."

"So, you won't even consider I speak the truth?"

"Anne." He edged up on one elbow, looked her in the eyes. "I dinnae wish lies between us. There's no need for it."

"Which is why I've decided to tell you the truth." She cupped his cheeks, leaned in and kissed him. "I truly am from the future, but I understand if you don't believe me. Maybe in time, you will."

"Your words dinnae always make sense, but these less than any other. I'll hear no more of this nonsense."

She wouldn't push him. Speaking the truth had lightened her heart, no matter his answer. Instead she kissed him again.

He moaned and she writhed against him. Such sweet agony. He returned her kisses, and she accepted the full length of his cock and the pounding rhythm of his sensual thrusts.

Time. Surely all it would take was a little time.

Chapter 4

As the dawn hour neared, Alex stirred and dragged himself out of bed. Anne remained curled on her side under the sheets, an enticement he had to leave behind. She certainly deserved her rest after last night. He hadn't been able to cease making love to her, as if every moment counted.

He dressed quickly before he succumbed and returned to her. His men would be waiting for a hard day of training after such revelry the day before. Downstairs at the edge of the great hall, he halted next to Alan, his trusted man.

"Alex, I didnae expect to see you so early." Alan scratched underneath his chin as he arched one thick red brow. "How is your wee bride this fine morn?"

"Abed, and no' to be disturbed." He crossed his arms. "Has there been any word from Fergus?"

"Nay, and he took Hawk." Hawk, their carrier pigeon, would be sent home once Fergus had sufficient word to convey.

"Good. Then report to me the moment Hawk returns." He clapped Alan on the back then continued to the dais and broke his fast with a steaming bowl of porridge and honey.

His men were jovial, eager to get outside and practice and he yearned to do the same. He rose, and his warriors scraped their chairs back and joined him. They moved in a steady stream out toward the yard.

* * * *

"Anne. There you are." Mary lifted her teal skirts and hurried along the passageway toward her.

She'd only taken one step out of Alex's chamber. "Good morning, Mary."

"Aye, 'tis good. How did you sleep?"

"Very well." She cleared her throat and smiled. "Thank you for the gowns you left atop Alex's trunk. I found them when I woke. How was your sleep?"

"Peaceful. James left for Dunvegan this morn to deliver news of your handfast. MacLeod will soon know our feud has been set aside." She smoothed out the lower ruffles of Anne's skirts then stood. "This deep blue matches your eyes to perfection. I thought it would. Come, it's nearly midday and so lovely outside. We'll gather flowers for the tables."

"I'm allowed beyond the gates?"

"You're kin now, so aye."

She followed Mary downstairs. This was what she'd come to Scotland for, to find family and to tour the countryside. Now she had both, and all at the same time. Overwhelming, yet wonderfully so. "Thank you, Annie," she whispered under her breath.

At the door, they collected two woven baskets and with them looped over their arms, walked out into the sunshine. The fresh sea air fully awakened her. "I can't believe how beautiful this place is. I thought it so cold to start with."

"What do you mean? To start with?" Mary linked her free arm through hers and they passed under the arch and headed toward the drawbridge.

"Oh, just that I enjoy when the season changes."

"As do I." She called out to the burly guardsman who shadowed them. "Good morn, Alan. Why do you follow us?"

He marched to their side. "My lady, the men practice this way."

"As they have for all the years I've known them to." Mary giggled. "Anne and I willnae disturb them. We need to fill these baskets. When the chief returns, I want every room awash in welcome."

"I will still watch over ye."

"We dinnae require protection on our land, or at least no' this close to the castle."

He grunted. "No wandering farther than the meadow. I'll keep an eye out."

"Come, Anne. The wildflowers await." She tugged her over the stone walled bridge, murmuring, "'Tis a grand sight if you wish to see the men training. They battle hard."

"Where are they?"

"Beyond the outbuildings near the shore where there is a goodly amount of flat land."

"I see." A great cloud of dust rose from that direction. They followed the meandering trail scattered with rocks, passed children playing near the stables. Uphill, they climbed, and at the top, Anne raised a hand to her brow. Stunning. Dunscaith sat at the mouth of Loch Eishort, and the waters shimmered blue-green from this vantage point. James would certainly have favorable conditions as he sailed to Dunvegan Castle along the coast.

"The Cuillin mountains look majestic today." Mary plucked several flowers from within the lush green grass.

"Yes." The mountains rose majestically. Wispy clouds dotted the horizon, floating toward the home of her ancestors. She was descended from the direct MacLeod bloodline, and that had never been more obvious than when Annie had stood before her. Theirs surely was fairy blood, for such a wish to come true.

Oh, but Dunvegan. How she'd love to visit the stronghold of her ancestors. She'd intended to go, determined to see it all by traveling the entire length of Skye.

Now, in the most unique way, that wish had come true.

"Mum, Dad, I wish you could be here," she murmured.

If only that were—oh my goodness. She was living in the past, and well before the time her parents had been taken.

Would it be possible for her to alert them of the danger ahead?

Her heartbeat raced. Why not?

This could be the reason she'd come, and not simply because of Annie's wish. Maybe she could leave her parents a message, one that warned them ahead of time of the fire that would take their lives.

Only how could she do that? New Zealand was a long way away and she still had no idea what year she'd arrived in.

"Anne, come and join me."

She spun and faced Mary. "I know this will sound strange, but indulge me. What year is it?"

"Oh, Anne." She laughed. "You are such a delight."

Delight aside, she had to know. "Do you believe the world is flat?"

Her giggles continued. "Nay. Men have sailed far and wide and have no' fallen off the sides. And there is the moon. Surely you've seen the roundness of it? Why would the Earth no' be so?"

"Rrright." She slapped her forehead. The moon was round. Geez, where had she heard about people believing the world had been flat?

So what time had she ended up in? From the brochure she'd read during her trip here, Dunscaith had been abandoned by the clan around sixteen-hundred and eighteen when the current chief had received a royal charter of the lands in the far north of Skye at Trotternish. Whatever time this was, it had to be prior to that.

If only the chief's name wasn't Donald MacDonald. Every chief she could recall from this clan had been named such.

"Are you going to help or stand there looking perplexed all

afternoon?"

"I'll help." She picked flowers until both their baskets overflowed. As they cut a path back to the castle she asked, "Has there been any word on the chief?"

"Nay, but Fergus will find him." Mary tugged on their linked arms, changed their course toward the dust cloud. "Pick up your pace, otherwise Alan will see us and bring our next adventure to a close."

"We're going to watch the warriors?"

"Aye, all that braw muscle needs appreciation, and at four and forty, I'm no' too old to enjoy the display."

Her heart lightened at Mary's words. "I would like to see Alex training."

"Oh, my Alex is very lucky to have found you."

"Hardly found, more like foisted upon."

She swatted her hand. "Shush, I shall hear no more talk of that."

They rounded the corner of the stables. Before the waters of the glistening loch, a hundred shirtless warriors wielded claymores in a battle of strength against one another.

She searched through the half-naked men and found the very one she was after. Alex's body was hard and packed with muscle, his shoulders and arms thick and strong. His chest held the finest smattering of hair, the same blond of his head. Below the plains of his glorious chest, his abs rippled, layer upon tight layer and all covered with a healthy sheen of sweat.

"He's by far the tallest." And Anne wanted every inch of that body back against hers.

"Aye, my son could never be missed in a battle."

His powerful form was magnificent, and his command of the warriors he fought against a sight to behold.

Alex thrust his enormous sword against his opponent's as if it were an extension of his arm and not a monstrous piece of steel. Now, this was exactly how he'd come about every one of those bulging muscles.

"I have to get closer." She passed Mary her basket.

"I'll hold Alan off."

"Thank you. You make a wonderful friend." Stepping forward, she focused on the man who'd made love to her so intensely throughout the night. He moved deftly, growing stronger with each strike of his claymore upon his opponent's blade.

The two men circled each other, as if waiting to pounce for the next attack. Alex raised his weapon and—

"Lass, get back here now." Alan tried to pass Mary who zigzagged in front of him.

"Damn," Alex swore, barely missing his challenger's blow. His gaze speared toward her. "What are you doing out here?"

She stared at his wide chest. Even the veins on his arms stood rigid and firm. "Sorry, the view was rather distracting."

"You could get hurt." He marched toward her, caught her arm then led her to the rear of the stables where all was quiet. "Lass, you cannae look at me like that."

"Like what?" She touched his chest with her finger then swirled down over his wicked abs.

"Like that." He picked her up, kicked open the door of a side room, set her down and slammed the door shut. His eyes burned a molten hue even in the dark confines of the cramped room. "Up with your skirts."

"What?"

"Up. With. Your." His plaid rose at the front, and all of its own accord.

"Oh, like that?"

He backed her against the wall. "Aye, like that."

"That's very clever." She grinned and finished lifting the soft tartan. Since he'd removed his trews to train, his legs were bare underneath. His cock was hard and held a glistening drop on the end. "Do you ever tire?"

"It appears, no' with you."

"I think I can help." She knelt and encircled her hand around his heavy shaft.

"If you're about to—"

"Oh, I am." She licked the head then swirled her tongue around it. Perfect. She opened her mouth and took as much of him in as she could. He tasted divine, salty and strong, and as she sucked, he groaned and rocked his hips.

* * * *

Alex couldn't speak. She settled her soft lips around him then pulled him in as deep as she could take. She'd unman him if he permitted much more. "Mercy."

"I don't think so." She sucked even harder.

"Nay, I want inside of you, no' to come in your pretty mouth." He pulled out. Hell, that had been the hardest thing he'd ever done. Yet harder still was his cock. He tumbled her to the floor, flipped her skirts then pulled her on top of him. "Ride me, and dinnae stop."

"Yes, sir." She gasped as she moved up and down. "Ohh, yesss, sir."

"I'm going to lose my mind."

"I want you to lose more than that." She arched her back as she picked up speed.

The intensity of the moment shook him. Grasping her hips, he rocked them harder until her tight channel hugged him all the way to his balls.

"Alex, I'm—"

"Let go. I'm right here with you."

"Oh, oh yes." She cried out as she pulsed around him.

With no choice, he came hard, shattering right along with her.

"Ahh, wonderful," she murmured then drooped on top of him.

"More like magnificent." He couldn't move. 'Twas as if

she'd drained his life's blood, and not on the battlefield, but the dusty floor of the stables. She wielded such control over him. "Sorry, my sweet."

"What's wrong?"

"I didnae mean for that to happen again, to come inside you."

"It's fine." Her eyelashes fluttered up. "I have something inside me which prevents pregnancy. I meant it when I said there won't be a child."

"And as I've told you, 'tis impossible."

"I know you did. Believe what you will, but I've no wish to lie to you." She ran her thumb over his lower lip then leaned in and kissed him.

"I cannae allow such a mistake again." Never had he lost his thoughts as he did with her. "Mayhap we should abstain. I dinnae seem to be able to keep my promise as I—"

She pressed her fingers over his mouth. "I don't know how long I'll be here, but while I am, I want to be your wife in all ways. I mean it."

"You'll be here a year."

"Sometimes things happen outside of our control."

"You may have slipped out of MacLeod's grasp, but you willnae slip out of mine." He rolled them and stood. "We need to talk, and you will speak of how you arrived here unescorted. This time, I'll have the truth."

* * * *

After straightening her clothing, Anne walked inside the keep with Alex leading the way. Great. How could she make him believe her?

"After you." He opened his chamber door.

She trudged inside. "I don't know what to say that I haven't already."

"We're no' leaving here until I have the truth." He crossed to the side table under the window and poured water from the jug into the basin.

"I've told you the truth, but you won't believe me."

"Dinnae speak of coming from the future and I will." He removed his plaid, soaked a cloth and washed his face and body until only the spicy scent of his soap lingered in the air. His wet skin gleamed and she itched to trace his golden skin. Too soon he covered himself with a clean shirt and trews, then tapped his foot. "I'm waiting. I'd never harm you."

"I know you wouldn't." To the unexplainable depths of her heart, the knowledge was clear in her mind. "All right. I'll start with the Fairy Flag, the powerful talisman of the MacLeod clan. Have you heard of it?"

"The MacLeods have fairy blood. That is the legend they tell. Apparently their Fairy Flag holds mystical powers."

"It does." She rubbed her damp palms against her skirts. "The flag is hidden somewhere at Dunvegan in this time, but in the future it's kept on display, or at least that's what I've heard."

"In this time?" His brows slashed down. "No' again."

"Ah, yes." She drew in a deep breath to fortify herself. "I'm not Anne MacLeod, or at least I am, but not the Anne MacLeod you believe me to be. I live in the future, in the year two-thousand and fourteen."

"You're speaking nonsense." Arms crossed, he snapped, "I want the truth, no' some fairy tale."

"It is the truth. I came here through a portal the night you returned from your search. I'd booked a tour to visit Dunscaith's ruins, and I was clinging to the drawbridge's ledge when the hole opened. James pulled me through, from my time to yours. I swear it's the truth."

"You'd already been here a sennight. Stop with the lies."

"That was Annie who was here. I'm directly descended from her, and we look exactly alike. Annie is the one who first made the wish upon the Fairy—"

"Nay, no more lies." He ground his heel against the floor.

"Give me the truth."

"In truth I live around the other side of the world, in a country as yet undiscovered." Since she'd begun, she might as well lay out all the facts. "In the 1850s ships sailed from England, taking men, women and children to settle in the newly discovered land of New Zealand. That's where my ancestors traveled to."

"Right, and somehow you sailed right back here again?"

"No, in my time one can catch a plane. You board it and the machine takes off and flies across the sky."

He snorted. "You have a wild imagination."

"If only I did. I promise you, many amazing things happen in the future, and Annie traveled there. When she visited Dunvegan in the future and looked upon the Fairy Flag, she was transported back to the past. She ended up here a week before I did. That's how she arrived unescorted, and I spoke to her. The night I arrived was the night she was pulled back."

"Pulled back to—" He shoved up his hand. "Cease. I've heard enough of this drivel and I shouldnae be encouraging you."

"You wanted the truth, Alex, and this is it. I don't know how long I'll be here. Annie disappeared before my eyes and I don't know what caused her to go. The same could happen to me and there is nothing I can do about it."

He speared her a fierce look then stormed to the door. He stood, his hand on the doorknob as if he didn't know whether he should stay or go. "I never want to hear you spout such rot again."

"I said you wouldn't believe me, but it isn't rot. I have no reason to lie to you."

"You're no' from the future."

"I am. In my time we have machines which do almost everything. Man no longer travels by horse, but within large steel contraptions that roll on wheels. Man has even taken one of those planes I spoke of, specially outfitted for space, and landed on the moon."

"Enough." He shook with fury.

"We have medications which prevent so many diseases and death. Women rarely die in childbirth and people live to eighty, ninety, even one hundred years of age."

"I cannae listen to any more of this. You're to remain here until I return." He yanked open the door and slammed it behind him. His booted footsteps clomped down the passageway.

Ooo-kay, that went well.

This time was so backward. He had no right to demand she remain here, only for the life of her, she wasn't game enough to open that door and step out.

She crossed to his corner desk. In the top drawer, she found paper, a quill and ink. Lovely. She sat in his chair and penned precise instructions for her parents to ensure they were never taken from her by the fire. The fire report had said the blaze had begun in their bedroom due to an electrical fault with their heater.

She listed the date and gave as much information as she could about her trip to the past, the very one Alex had not believed her of. But her parents had to. At the end of the note, she signed her name then blew on the ink until it dried. After folding it in three, she tucked it into an envelope and sealed it with red wax and the MacDonald stamp.

Now, she had to get this to the MacLeod stronghold. Dunvegan had never fallen to another clan, and it was the one place in the future where someone might ensure her letter was kept safely locked away. Her parents had to receive this note, and before they perished. Surely they'd believe her.

Her heart throbbed and sank like a stone in her chest. She wanted more time with Alex, but if she was pulled back to her own time before she'd had a chance to deliver this letter then she'd never forgive herself.

* * * *

Cursing, Alex marched into the great hall. Dunscaith would never fall into ruin. Anne could not possibly have come from the future, and all those things she'd spouted couldn't even conceivably occur.

"What has that dark look on your face, my son?" His mother wandered around the trestle tables, placing bowls of arranged flowers in the center of each one. Other than her, the room was clear, still he couldn't repeat his wife's words. They might turn his mother against her. Although, Mother had been here as he had not.

"'Tis naught. Have you noticed a difference in Anne since the night she escaped?"

She halted then fidgeted with a bowl. "While you were gone, she was amenable, but neither of you had spent much time with each other. I feared she was uncertain, so before your handfast, we spoke. All was well afterward."

"She did no' appear different?"

Water sloshed from the next bowl as she placed it on the table. Her gaze jumped to his. "Pray tell what you mean by different?"

He had to be careful he didn't raise her suspicions. "I only meant by her disposition."

"Oh, then aye, but she is a MacLeod among so many MacDonalds. Her earlier wariness while you were away was expected." She took the last bowl and walked to the stairs. "I must finish seeing to the flowers. The chambers need brightening. I'll see you at the evening meal."

"You will." He had already lost much of his afternoon, and the loch awaited.

Outside, converged at the edge of the shore, his men stripped off their shirts and rolled their trews to their knees. He did the same then dove into the loch and led the way. They swam several miles along the coast as part of their daily training.

Swimming such distances was imperative since they fought on both land and sea. It ensured they were at their fittest. Any possible weakness could certainly lead to death, and a warrior's life was already short enough.

As dark descended, he slogged out of the water, pulled his shirt on and a dry pair of trews left by one the maids. Dressed, he tramped to the keep. His men followed, their hungry rumblings heard by the maids who rushed to fill the tables with hot and hearty dishes of food and their tankards with ale.

With his clan assembled in the great hall, he took his place at the dais and turned to Alan at his right. "Do you have aught to report?"

"Your lady has kept to your chamber since ye left."

Good. At least she had not defied his order. He removed the dirk strapped to his thigh, stabbed a wedge of beef and ate it from the tip.

"Good evening, Alex." His mother swished by and took her seat. "Where is Anne?"

"Abed."

"Oh, still? Is she well?"

"Aye, she's well." He filled his trencher with steaming food, enough for him and Anne. Her insistence she was from another time had plagued him during his swim. Such a thing wasn't possible and the responsibility of setting her to rights fell to him. "I shall see she has food. Goodnight, Mother."

"Sleep well, and give Anne a kiss for me."

He almost smiled at her need to interfere. What was he going to do with his wife? And what had truly caused her lone arrival here? He entered his chamber and shut the door. In bed, Anne lay awake under the covers, her long hair spread across her pillow and his. "I brought you food."

"Thanks." She edged up onto her elbows and scrutinized him. "I forgive you by the way. It took a bit of time, but I guess you have the right to be dubious."

"Nay, no more of this nonsense." He set the food on the bedside table, shucked his clothes and climbed in. He'd forbid her to speak of this if he must, even with him.

"Where I come from, women speak freely, we even vote."

"I for—"

"We marry whom we wish, and usually without interference from our family. Women even work inside and outside the home, bringing the bacon home just as the men do."

"Now I know you lie."

"It's quite acceptable for women to have children outside of wedlock." She stroked the area between his brows. "Look at this frown. I truly wish you'd believe."

"'Tis impossible to believe such a thing, and from now on you'll no' utter another word. Do you understand?"

"I can't allow this opportunity to pass. My parents died in my time, but three years past. I've written them a letter and I have to get it to Dunvegan. The castle has remained the stronghold of the chiefs of MacLeod for over eight-hundred years."

Obviously he'd no' spelled it—nay, she'd written a letter?

"Anne, are you saying your chief saw you learned to read and write?"

"All children have a right to an education. In the future."

"I didnae mean in the future." Why would she not relent on this?

"I majored in accounting and spent three years at university, although we hardly have the need to write in my time. We use slim devices the size of your trencher, which have all the letters and numbers set as keys on a wide pad. You enter the written word in and it shows up on a bright screen before you. You can then send what you've written to yet another device closer to the size of Mary's basket. It stamps your words onto paper, or you can simply send it anywhere in the world to the person you need to, like a letter."

"What the?" Hell, her imagination was rife.

"One's message can also move from one device to another across any distance, no matter if they're not linked. Contacting someone is immediate."

Certain his jaw hung somewhere down in his lap, he stared at her. Rife didn't even begin to describe her imagination. "So you're saying you dinnae need a messenger?"

She smiled, and he could have slapped himself for encouraging her further. "No, and that's not the only means of communication. Almost everyone in the world has a land or cell phone. With those you simply press a button and—"

"Stop." He was digging himself in deeper. He had to halt her spiel. Now. "You have the ability of a bard who weaves the most intriguing tales, but tales they are."

"You truly want me to stop?"

"Aye, and to never start again."

"What of my letter? I have to get it to Dunvegan."

"There is no need for such when you didnae come from the future."

"But what if I did?" Her gaze pleaded with him. "What if I'm taken from you? I mean here, before I've done what I must do. For years I've wished I could change the past, and now with Annie's wish it's possible." She caught his hands. "My parents deserve to live."

"You are no' alone. You have me."

"I want my wish to come true as Annie's did. I need to journey to Dunvegan."

* * * *

Even with all Alex's decrees of denial, he was still listening to her. "I need you if I'm ever to get to Dunvegan. Please, Alex, take me there."

"The feud between our clans will only settle once MacLeod hears of our handfast. I've sent James."

"Then take me once James returns."

"Nay, there is no reason for me to allow such a visit unless at your request. MacLeod will believe I have a weakness for you."

"But you don't."

"Aye, it seems I do. Even now I seek to plunder what's beneath your nightrail." He cupped her breasts through the thin ivory cotton.

Warmth flooded her below and she swayed into him. "I have a weakness for you too, and you will drive me mad if you don't satisfy this hunger."

"We have a year, and I intend to see you're well and truly sated by the end of it." He dipped his head and sucked on one nipple, drawing both it and the cloth into his mouth.

Hot. Her Highlander knew how to kiss. "Where I come from the newly married honeymoon. They don't leave their bed for days or even weeks on end. Can we do that?"

"I can give you naught but my nights." With his teeth, he tugged her front lacings loose until her breasts spilled out. He licked his lips. "You've already stolen me from my training this day. It cannae happen again."

"So, you're saying no?"

"I will see to your needs now." He swiped his tongue over one nipple then the other. "And mine. I must have more." He wriggled her nightrail down and she kicked it away.

The candlelight flickered over his impressive erection bobbing against the rippling contours of his abs. "I have a feeling you're about to become my weakness too."

He lowered to the curve of her neck and kissed her. "Your heartbeat flutters like the wings of a bird. We will indulge, though only here. Do you understand?"

"Yes." He kissed down the valley of her breasts and over her belly. She shivered in delight. "Provided you keep doing that."

"I give you my word I shall. I'm hungry and a feast awaits."

He spread her legs, revealing all of her to his savage gaze.

A thrill chased through her and she slid her legs against his.

"Beautiful." He ducked his head and she tangled her hands in his thick golden hair. She held onto him as his tongue swept across her flesh.

A firestorm radiated out from where he touched, and then he moved his mouth over her sensitive clit, and sucked, hard.

Breathless, she clung to him. "Slow down. What happened to *we had all night?*"

"You hold the banquet of my dreams." Licking her, he built her orgasm to such a height she'd never manage the downhill return. "Let yourself go, my sweet. I want to feel you come with my mouth."

She lifted her hips and her legs fell wider.

He drank from her deeper, his demand growing more frenzied as he grasped her bottom and moaned. This was heaven, and she never wanted their time together to end, not now, and not in a year. Having nowhere to go but over the edge, she arched her back and exploded. Flashes of white burst behind her closed eyelids as she came, over and over. Breathing in the elixir of his spicy scent, she clutched him to her. It was too much, yet not enough. "I want you inside."

"Aye, I need that too." He rose over her.

"Hurry." She wanted to feel every hard and pulsing inch of him.

Lust filled his gaze. "Did I no' sate you even a little?"

"Not by half." She wrapped her arms around his neck, molded herself to him and gave him the friction he adored. "I'm not sure you ever will."

"That was no' the answer I was after."

"I meant you did." She nipped his lower lip. "But I want more."

"You are bold."

"Twenty-first century women are. We know what we want

and we take it. Don't ever expect docility from me, not with the passion you've now unleashed."

"I dinnae care for docility." He took control of their kiss, his hunger for her mouth matching his ravenous need of before. He thrust his tongue between her lips then plundered and pillaged with each mind-bending stroke.

His passion was endless, but then so was hers. She certainly could never have imagined she'd want her handfast husband this much. Yes, her husband and no one else's. Her heartbeat pounded. "Don't ever let me go, Alex. I want you, all of you. Make me yours."

He clasped her hips and slowly moved his cock between her legs. The thick head teased her entrance as he slid himself along her dampness. "You were mine the moment we spoke our vows. No one will ever take you from me."

Before she drew in her next breath, he plunged into her. Her scream was smothered by his mouth.

"Feel me in you," he moaned as he pulled out then slid fully back home. "How we belong together. Dinnae take your lips from mine."

She kissed him as feverously as he kissed her. He filled her, everywhere, claiming all of her. Then he quickened his pace and thrust harder and deeper. His strokes were masterful, and she pushed her hips toward him as her inner muscles grasped and dragged him home.

"Anne, damn." He grit his teeth and held himself stiff as she pulsed around him.

"Don't." She rocked underneath him. "Come with me."

He looked deep into her eyes then roared as he sank balls-deep into her. His seed shot to her womb and she cried out at their shared climax. A more perfect moment she'd never known. Joined together, it was a connection she never wanted to break.

Finally her breathing settled and the fevered speed of her heartbeat slowed. He rolled off her, taking her with him to lie on top. Their limbs remained tangled, and she snuggled against him. "Okay, now I'm well sated, honey."

He tightened his hold on her, his voice raspy as he said, "Well, I still have some way to go. Prepare yourself for a battle like no other. I wish to conquer this desire, or at least for this eve."

"Oh, I've unleashed the warrior within." She caressed his chest. "And I hope you never submit to defeat."

Yes, did she wish.

Chapter 5

Alex slipped out of their room the next morn and strode downstairs to the great hall. Alan beckoned him from near the private side room. He crossed and followed his man inside. "You have news?"

"Aye. This just arrived. A message from Fergus." He passed him a small roll of tattered paper.

He unraveled it and read. "Nay, it cannae be."

"'Tis bad news?"

"Fergus came upon one of the king's messengers sent to impart this news to us. Our chief is in Edinburgh, along with his brother, Angus MacDonald of Dunnyveg."

Alan thumped the center table covered in the seneschal's accounts. "The chief would no' willingly travel there, no' at this time."

"I agree." Some months ago, a missive had arrived from the king, requesting their chief present himself at court to atone for his feuding with the MacLean of Duart. Donald expected all those involved in the dispute had received the same request. To travel to Edinburgh would mean his capture and imprisonment. Uncle would never take such a risk.

"The king needs to leave us to resolve our own issues, no'

alter the way we settle our disputes." Alan clenched his fists.

"Aye, but he wishes to stamp his mark of ownership on the Western Isles, to control our way of life." He returned to the missive. "Fergus reports he will continue onto Edinburgh and find out all he can. He'll send word in due course."

"What will you tell the clan?"

"The truth." They would be aware soon enough of what had transpired. Secrets were difficult to keep within these walls, and the news their chief had been captured by the king's men wasn't information he wished to withhold, not even for a short time.

* * * *

Anne stretched then recoiled at the chill coming from Alex's side of the bed. The sheets were cold, as if he'd left some time ago. She squinted through the dark. A sliver of dawn light snuck through the wooden-shuttered window. Her warrior must have gotten up early.

Curling into a tighter ball, she held onto the remaining heat. Last night had been wonderful, although no matter her plea for him to take her to Dunvegan, he'd still given her an adamant no.

His "no" though, wouldn't cut it, not when her parents' lives were at stake. Which meant action. She couldn't lie abed when she had a letter to deliver, somehow and someway.

She shoved the covers away and planted her feet on the icy floor. Oh, some carpet on the polished planks would be nice. Across the room, she hopped. She hauled the engraved lid of the trunk up and selected one of the dresses Mary had delivered that first morning.

"Anne?" A knock sounded on the door. "I brought more clothes."

"Oh, come in."

She bustled in with an array of colorful garments spilling over her arms. She heaved the pile onto the end of the bed and faced her. "I've brought a special treat too."

"You did? You better mean woolen socks."

Grinning, she plucked a pair of stockings free. "Close. Put them on, and I'll help you dress. We're going outside shortly."

"But it's still dark."

"We have to leave with the men when they do, otherwise we miss out." She rummaged through the pile then yanked a forest-green riding habit and a broad-brimmed hat out. "We're going riding. Alex has organized a hunt to restore our reserves. The men are eager to leave."

"I love riding, although I've never been on a hunt. That sounds wonderful." Mary held out a white shirt for her to don under the fitted jacket. The riding habit's skirt was long and full, quite cumbersome and weighty, but it would allow her to ride astride. "I can't believe Alex is allowing me to go."

"You're safe here and we'll be hunting on our lands. It didnae take much persuading when I asked. Wait here though while I change. I willnae be long." She skipped out the door.

A maid bobbed her head and entered with a tray brimming with food. She thanked the young girl, ate the porridge and one of the delicious oatcakes. The letter. No matter what, she'd keep it on her. It was best to remain prepared.

Mary returned, outfitted in a burgundy riding habit trimmed with navy ribbon, and a hairbrush in hand. "I'll help with your hair. 'Tis tangled something fierce."

"Thank you. Where do you usually hunt?"

"North. Deep in the forest." She detangled the length then wound it up high and pinned it in place. Next, she eased the wide hat overtop and adjusted it on an angle. "I learnt to shoot with the bow and arrow alongside my brothers when I was young. I enjoy a good hunt, taking down a pesky wolf, or felling a prized deer."

"Is it difficult to wield the weapon?"

"No' if one practices." She tied the ribbons underneath her chin. "Having you here is wonderful. I've missed my daughter terribly since she left, and she never missed a hunt."

"And I've missed having a mother figure." She hugged Mary extra hard as the truth of her words hit home. "Alex is lucky to have you."

"He's a good son, and a strong, caring leader. This morn in the great hall, he reported word had come from Fergus. The chief has been taken by the king's men to Edinburgh."

"What? Why?"

"It all started in fifteen-hundred and eighty-five. Five years past, the chief sailed to visit his brother, the MacDonald of Dunnyveg. During the trip he and his men were forced to shelter in Jura. Bad weather and all. Unfortunately they landed on the MacLean of Duart's portion of the island, and that night came under attack. We lost almost sixty men because of MacLean. 'Tis a vicious feud which rages there."

"What does that mean for the chief?"

"Imprisonment, although Fergus continues onto Edinburgh and will send further news once he has it."

Alex would be devastated, as would the clan. "I'm so sorry. What happens now?"

"Another of Donald's nephews, no' Alex, is the first to succeed should the chief's imprisonment lead to death, but he's still a lad. Alex will lead until Donald returns."

Goodness, she finally had a date, fifteen-ninety, which meant the king Mary spoke of was James VI, the man who would unite the kingdoms of England and Scotland in sixteen-hundred and three. He wasn't a king to forget.

She'd traveled to a time of war within the isles, but also to a time where history would be made. She'd come to Scotland, and Dunscaith's ruins because her clan too had resided here. Of course, the MacDonalds had lived here for far longer. If only she'd read more within that brochure. "I don't know what will happen, Mary."

"It's all right, lass. No one knows the future, but the chief is strong. He'll return to us."

She gripped Mary's hands. "It can't be his time."

Nor was this hers, although all roads led to Dunvegan. Her letter must be delivered into the Chief of MacLeod's hands for safekeeping.

Her parents' future survival depended on her, and she wouldn't let them down.

"Of course the chief willnae die. You sound like a MacDonald. Come." She smiled and tugged her from the room. "We dinnae want the men to leave without us."

* * * *

A hunt was exactly what his men needed to clear their heads after the devastating news Alex had given them. He checked his destrier's saddle and tightened the cinch.

"Alex, wait for us." Mother rushed toward him, and one step behind her, Anne hurried with her hands bunched in her skirts. She'd lifted them a tantalizing inch above her ankles, displaying a sliver of delicious flesh.

"Anne, come here. Mother has her own mare."

Her chest rose and fell enticingly under her fitted jacket. "I'm riding with you?"

He offered her his hand. "I wish to keep you close during the hunt."

"I'd rather ride my own horse." She squeezed his hand. "Please."

"Nay." He mounted then drew her up in front of him. Damn, this close, she was a total distraction, her heavenly scent firing his need for her.

She half turned toward him then slapped his chest. "Hey, you shouldn't look at me like that. Your mother is right there."

"You're a temptation I never expected."

"And you are a nuisance, even though an adorable one. Get this horse moving."

Chuckling, he nudged his horse's flanks. "I've never been called adorable."

"Because that's my job to state so." She adjusted her skirts then gasped as they rode beyond the moors and into the forest. "The colors of the trees are beautiful. It must still be autumn even though winter is close. What month is it?"

"You still believe you're from the future and dinnae know the month or year?"

"It's fifteen-ninety. Mary told me." Her cheeks flushed as he rode deeper along the hunting trail. "Please, tell me. What month is it?"

She was so insistent she came from the future. Last night, he'd even found himself swaying a touch when he didn't fully discourage her talk of it. Even now, his mouth opened as if to spill what she wished to hear.

"Oooh, you're almost there." She rubbed her bottom against his groin. "Come on. I'll reward you later if you tell me."

His cock hardened. His bride was such a tease. "'Tis late October, and my reward shall be sought the moment we return to the castle."

"You have a deal." She eased the back of her head onto his shoulder. "Wouldn't it be wonderful to make love outside in a secluded meadow? Since you're so big and warm, I probably wouldn't even feel the cold."

"Anne." His cock jabbed into her lower back. Not a tease, but a tormenter. "We're on a hunt, with a score of men."

"I wanted you to know how much I crave your company too. Life is short, and I've been without anyone for so long. Now I have you, even though my future is so uncertain." She patted her pocket. "I brought the letter, and this probably isn't the right time to speak of it, but I can't give up on my quest to get this missive to the Chief of MacLeod. I'll always keep it on me should you change your mind. Annie did mention she couldn't defy Rory, and now I'm aware of the year, that would make her cousin and chief Roderick MacLeod. He's a legend in the history books, and known as Rory. He even marries a MacDonald, although not for a few more years. I think. I studied what I could before I traveled."

"There isnae a chance Rory MacLeod will wed a MacDonald. He will seek an alliance elsewhere, where he can expand on his lands. And we spoke vows. You will remain as my wife, regardless of what you say."

"You're a stubborn man, although I'm glad I handfasted with you, and that it wasn't Annie."

"As am—" He shook his head. "I mean—"

"I would love it if you believed me, but it's enough you're not locking me away. Your reward just doubled. Now let's enjoy the hunt. Will I get to use the bow and arrow?"

"Mother is a fine teacher."

"You won't teach me?"

"Nay, I will only want to drag you behind the bushes and have my wicked way with you. We'll water the horses soon, and you can take some time to practice with Mother's bow." He wanted more than his wicked way, and her idea of making love in a meadow, would happen as soon as he could arrange it.

* * * *

"The arrow needs to arch before hitting its target, so allow for a higher degree of aim." Mary stepped back from Anne and nodded. "You can do it."

"You're a patient teacher." Alex had wet and slapped a mound of moss into the crook of an ash tree, a good thirty feet away. Four guardsmen remained with them in the clearing near the stream where they'd stopped. Though Alex had left soon after their arrival, taking the remainder of his men with him to begin the hunt. "When will Alex be back?"

"Soon. Focus on your target. He will want to see you can hit it afore he allows you to try and take down a rabbit or other small animal."

She placed her cheek to the side of the arrow as she pulled the bowstring back, and then carefully, she lifted the arrow tip a fraction and let it go. It flew free, arching beautifully as it sailed. On her tiptoes, she followed its flight until it speared the mossy mound dead center. "I did it." She jumped in a dizzying circle.

Mary clapped and beamed. "That's perfect. Now you must practice for an hour each day, and build your skill."

"I wish Alex had seen that."

"I will tell him. Oh, listen. I hear horses." She cocked her ear then shot a worried look at Alan. "They're moving at speed."

The pounding hooves became deafening, as if dozens of horses thundered down the trail.

"Mary," Alan called. "Take Anne and wait within the trees." He and the other guardsmen stationed around the perimeter mounted their horses and moved into a tight group.

"Come." Mary dragged her into the woods and shoved her behind a thick trunk. "Shh, no' a word."

She peeked through the foliage. A roar went up as a score of warriors on horseback galloped into the clearing and pulled up before their guard.

Alan drew his claymore, eased his horse forward and addressed the man atop the largest destrier. "Rory MacLeod. You are some distance from your lands."

Leather trews hugged his thick legs and a buckskin vest molded his broad chest. His dark blond hair, tied with a strip of leather, trailed over the tip of a claymore holstered across his back. No wonder Rory MacLeod was a legend. His size alone stated it so.

"We've yet to reach Dunscaith, and here I find a party waiting within a meadow. Who have you been left to guard, MacDonald?"

"No one. We stopped to water our horses."

MacLeod eyed their mounts. "You must have stopped for some time. Your rides appear well-rested. Come, there's nay need to lie. I'm in your neck of the woods seeking my cousin. Annie disappeared, and we have scoured the isle and no' found her. Mayhap you have?"

"Or mayhap we have no'." Alan remained resolute in his stand, his weapon propped across his lap, but held firmly in hand. She didn't doubt he was ready to strike. Only why the lie? James had been sent to Dunvegan to inform the chief of hers and Alex's handfast. He should impart the truth now.

"The lass has blue eyes and hair of white-gold. She was promised in handfast to Alex MacDonald, though I had yet to bring her to him." MacLeod circled one finger in the air and his men followed his unspoken command and surrounded their guard. To his man on his right, he ordered, "Search the area for whom they protect, but dinnae harm them." To Alan, he said, "There's no need for bloodshed if my cousin is returned safely into my hands."

"You said yourself she was promised to Alex."

"Aye, but 'twas an agreement I had no choice to enter into because of your chief. If you have no' heard, he now enjoys the king's hospitality, within his dungeons. The contract between us is void. My cousin shall be returned to me."

Anne clutched Mary's hand. Oh, without Alex, she was a sitting duck. Although, not to her own clan. She dug into her pocket to ensure her parents' letter was safe.

This was her chance. "Mary, I need to go," she whispered. "I'm so sorry, but I have to."

"Nay." Mary seized her. "You're my daughter and Alex has become attached to you."

"These men are armed, and I won't have anyone harmed because I didn't step forward."

"Found her. There are two women." She jumped as a MacLeod guardsmen loomed over them. He offered her his hand. "Annie, come."

Mary bolted in front and pushed the man away. "She and my son have handfasted. You cannae take her away. She is Alex's wife by right."

"Mary, no." She grasped Mary's hands. "No bloodshed."

"You have to stay. Alex will fight this."

Which was what she didn't want. Alex getting hurt because of her wasn't an option. "I'm going. Tell him this was my choice."

"Once you leave Dunscaith and return to your kin, your handfast vow ends. You took Alex as your husband for the next year and a day, or until you no longer resided in his home. That was your vow."

"Is that right, Annie?" Rory MacLeod appeared and towered over her. "'Tis good to see you are well. I have feared for your safety."

"Roderick?" The legend stood before her.

He frowned. "Lass, am I in trouble because it took so long to find you?"

"Ah, no. I've been well looked after, Rory. Alex has been kind and considerate."

"Well, you need no' worry about him. You are back under my care. Come, we return now."

"Dinnae leave like this." Mary threw her arms around her.

She hugged Mary back. "I have to go. This is my chance."

"Ladies." Rory eased between them and set Mary to one side. "My apologies, Mistress MacDonald, but we must be away. Pass onto Alex my gratitude for his care of my cousin. The current sins of his chief are in no way reflected upon him."

"Alex willnae let this rest." Mary stood up to him.

"He has no choice. Anne is a MacLeod and their handfast has come to an end. You said yourself her vow will be broken once she leaves with me."

"If you take her, then allow me to visit." Mary clearly had no intention of backing down. "Anne and I have become exceedingly close."

Rory heaved a sigh as he turned his gaze on Anne. "You have a champion. I should no' be surprised."

"Can she visit? Please, Rory." Yes, she had to get his promise, to have hope she'd at least see Mary again.

He slowly nodded at Mary. "You're welcome at Dunvegan. My hospitality extends to you."

"Thank you." Her breath rushed out.

"Good day." Rory bowed, pressed his hand against Anne's back and steered her toward his horse. "I've searched for you everywhere, lass. This was the last place I expected to find you."

"It's the last place I expected to end up too."

"Your words sound strange."

"I—I—"

"Here. I'll give you a lift." Rory hoisted her onto his horse, slid in behind her and gripped the reins. He eyed Alan. "I appreciate the ease in which you've handed over Anne. Inform MacDonald their handfast is done." He nudged his horse's flanks and they rode out, his men following behind them.

Goodness, she'd done it. She had her letter in hand and now the ear of the MacLeod chief. Her accent was off, but she'd deal with it. She'd give anything to have her parents back.

Her spirits soared then quickly plummeted. Alex. If only she hadn't had to leave him like this, or so soon. Though he was still out here within this forest.

Autumn leaves lined the trail, and ash and elm trees grew tall either side. They rode for half an hour, until finally the ocean and its rhythmic crashing reached her on the breeze. No Alex. She missed him, but the task before her was set and he'd remain safer this way.

"I'm so sorry, Rory." She turned to the warrior behind her.

"You're safe and well. I only wish you hadn't left for Dunscaith as you did. The way things have turned out, 'twas an agreement I could have easily withdrawn from now the MacDonald of Sleat enjoys the king's accommodations."

"Alex was truly honorable."

"As you've said, although I have no intention of allowing

another match to occur between you and him. How did you sneak away without a guard?"

Now wasn't a good time to tell him when one of his men could overhear. No, she'd explain it all once they were alone. Only what excuse could she use? "I paid one of the villagers." That seemed plausible, hopefully.

He grunted. "Then that villager will be punished as nary a soul came forth to admit such." He drew his horse up along the shoreline. The waters of the loch glistened, and a birlinn rocked where it'd been partially beached. Two warriors waited near the vessel. "Stretch your legs but dinnae wander far. Dunscaith's village is over the rise, and I need only return these horses then we can set sail." He jumped to the ground then swung her down.

"Thank you." She scrambled along the rocky shoreline toward a small stream that ran into the loch. On her knees, she scooped water and splashed her face. What was Alex thinking? Surely he would know by now what had happened.

No, she couldn't think of Alex, not when she had a mission to complete.

She gripped the letter within her pocket. It had been easy enough to write, but now she had to convince Rory of where she'd come from, and that he held her parents' lives in his hands.

Would he listen when the time came?

* * * *

Damn. Alex had returned to find his mother in tears and his wife gone. He raised his sword and swung it at Alan. His man whipped his weapon up to counter his move. Their blades crashed, the violent clang booming across the meadow. "You let her go. I'll take your head off for it."

"I had no choice. Anne no longer resided within Dunscaith's walls, and we didnae need to aggravate MacLeod when we were so outnumbered. You should have wed her proper if you'd wanted more than what you'd spoken of in your vows."

"I never intended for MacLeod to get his hands on her." He

should never have brought them on this hunt.

"They left an hour ago and rode toward the shore." Alan sheathed his blade and mounted his horse. "We'll follow their tracks."

A guardsman hoisted Mother onto her horse. He wouldn't place her in any further danger. Alan had been right not to antagonize MacLeod with the women so near, yet he was in no mood to say so. "Mother, you'll have three escorts to take you home. No diverting from the path."

"MacLeod willnae hand her back, and they can reach the shore in half that time." She wiped her wet, blotchy cheeks. "I secured an invitation to Dunvegan."

"You did?" He rubbed his jaw.

An invitation. Hmm, he could retrieve his wife from right under MacLeod's nose if he played his cards well. Certainly he hadn't wished for anyone to see how much he cared for Anne, but his vow still stood, and he wouldn't allow it to fall.

He called out to his men, "We return to Dunscaith then sail for Dunvegan. I want my wife. Arm yourselves well."

Chapter 6

After almost two days of icy wind in her face and a night on the cold ground, the long sea journey to Dunvegan Castle was almost done. Anne huddled within a thick MacLeod plaid as Dunvegan rose like a fortress ahead, its massive gray towers and fortified walls topped with battlements and guardsmen roaming the ramparts. From the multitude of square windows, candlelight flickered in welcome.

Her clansmen plunged their oars into the depths, speeding their birlinn toward the sea-gate. So close.

"Not long, Annie," Rory called from his seat where he directed his men.

At the edge of the sea-gate, two large men waded into the water. Each seized a side of the birlinn as they came abreast of them. Hearty welcomes from the two warriors rang out as they guided the birlinn the last few feet and nestled it next to the stone stairs.

One of the men offered her his hand, and she grasped hold. "Watch your step, my lady. The rocks are slippery."

Her legs shook from being confined to one position for so long, but with his aid she climbed out. "Thank you."

Another warrior gripped her arm and kept her steady. His

eyes glinted with specks of yellow from the flickering torch he held. "Follow me."

He moved forward, the soft glow from his torch providing enough light to guide her along the rocky path winding upward. She slogged along, her feet frozen within her shoes.

Rory took her elbow as he caught her up. "You'll rest well tonight."

"Will I ever." She tramped through a darkened passageway and into an inner courtyard. Ahead, the stone entry of the keep beckoned.

She was here. Over four-hundred years in the past, but still, here.

Taking a deep breath, she slowly turned around. Her clansmen surrounded her. They stood tall and strong. "Thank you all for coming for me."

These men didn't know her, even though they presumed they did. Regardless, they were her kin. She blinked, pushing back tears. Home. She hadn't had one in so long.

"Annie!" A young woman tore from the keep, her pale hair billowing behind her. She darted through the men and wrapped arms fiercely around her. "I've missed you terribly. Where did you go? How did Rory find you? Are you—"

"Margaret, allow Annie inside before you begin questioning her so thoroughly." Rory ruffled Margaret's hair as if they shared a close bond.

Hmm, Annie had said if she hadn't agreed to the handfast, it would have been Margaret, Rory's sister who would have been bound to Alex.

"Have a bath drawn and a meal sent to her room," Rory continued. "Then you may catch up."

"Aye, I'm so sorry." Margaret looped her arm through Anne's then tugged her into the keep.

They entered the great hall, and the men she'd traveled with poured into the room behind her. Those at the tables rose and crowded around them, welcoming Rory, her and the men home. Margaret passed along Rory's order to one of the maids, then guided her through the throng of well-wishers and up the curved stairs to the second floor.

"I should have had your fire lit when I heard the call Rory's birlinn approached. I knew he'd found you. He promised he wouldnae return until he had." Margaret shoved open a chamber door. "Your journey must have been arduous. Where have you been?"

"At Dunscaith, with Alex MacDonald." Annie's chamber held a queen-sized bed with a thick canopy drawn around the sides. The rich blue velvet swept onto the polished wooden floors. Gorgeous.

"You were?" Clapping a hand to her mouth, she barely hid her gasp. "That must have been awful. When you first disappeared, Rory scoured the nearby countryside. No one saw you leave, nor was it time for my brother to deliver you to Alex MacDonald. How did you find your way there?"

"It's hard to—"

A maid hurried in and lit the fire. Two barefoot lads with sooty imprints on the knees of their breeches heaved a tub into the room. Another maid arrived with a drying cloth and bar of soap, and behind her another servant carried a tray. She set it on the side table then one-by-one they left.

"Never mind. Come and eat first. You can tell me everything once you have." Margaret held out a chair.

"Thank you. I'm so hungry." Breathing in the wonderful scent of mutton stew, she sat. A chunk of bread wedged half into it made her mouth water. She scooped it up and bit into it. The richly flavored juices exploded in her mouth. Delicious and hot. She ate until her belly could take no more.

"I'll remove your shoes." Margaret knelt, tugged her wet boots and soggy stockings free and dumped them in a pile. It had been impossible to keep her feet out of the sea-water sloshing in the boat's hull. "There we go."

The maids returned along with the boys, each carrying a steaming pail of water.

Margaret oversaw the filling of the tub then added a few drops of scented oil and a sprinkle of dried petals. "Perfect." She clapped her hands. "Everyone out."

They shut the door behind them.

"That looks amazing. Thank you." With the room now cozy and warm, she shed her dirty riding habit then sank into the glorious water.

"You sound different, but I've missed my favorite cousin. Rory was a bear after you first left. He scoured the woods, the village, hunted down any ruffians encamping on our land. He was sure someone had stolen you away. That you'd head for Dunscaith didnae cross his mind until the end. Would you like me to wash your hair?"

"No, but sit and talk with me." She slid under the water then emerged with a grin. "Oh, that is more than amazing."

Margaret laughed, her blue eyes sparkling. "Here, I shall help whether you wish it or no'. Your hair is matted something terrible." She lathered the soap then worked the suds through her hair. "Tell me all about Alex MacDonald. I saw him that time he came with his chief, but from afar."

"You mean when he signed the agreement?"

"Aye. Dip your head and rinse." She did, and after she popped up, Margaret carefully detangled her hair with a brush. "'Twas the meeting Rory asked you to attend, to ensure you had no issues with the handfast, though you didnae go."

"Oh, that meeting. My timing was out." By centuries no less. "I didn't mean to miss it."

"You certainly did." Margaret snorted. "How did you make the trip unescorted to Dunscaith? I'm surprised that's the path you chose. You told me divine intervention might be in order, and mayhap you'd even make a wish upon the Fairy Flag."

Perhaps Margaret was the one she needed, and not Rory. She hadn't yet had the chance to speak to him. She couldn't miss this opportunity. "I did wish upon it. Although not me exactly, but Annie."

"You are Annie." She plopped the brush down, wrapped her wet hair in a cloth then rubbed.

With an elbow on the edge of the tub, she faced Margaret. "It sounds as if you believe in the fairy blood within the MacLeod line?"

"All MacLeods do." She tapped her arm as if in reprimand. "Why would you ask such a silly question?"

"Because I'm Anne MacLeod, but not the Annie MacLeod you know. On the last full moon, Annie made a wish upon the Fairy Flag and asked to travel to a place where she wouldn't be forced to handfast with Alex. She told me a portal opened from this time to the future."

"I'm sorry, are you saying"—Margaret flicked a hand between them—"you're no' my cousin?"

"Yes, although I look just like her."

She smiled, rather indulgently. "Then how did you meet Annie, and how did you get here?"

"Your cousin was overcome with curiosity to see Dunvegan in its future form, and the moment she re-entered the great hall and looked upon the Fairy Flag, she was plucked from the future and returned to the past."

"I believe in the Fairy Flag, but no' that great of a tale." She tweaked her nose. "I'm no' a bairn anymore, Annie."

"It's not a tale. Annie returned to Dunscaith. She'd been there a week when I arrived through a portal from my time. She told me her wish both took and gave, but she promised to find a way to fix what she'd started. That was right before she disappeared before my eyes."

"And where did she go that time?"

"I don't know. Finding out what happened to her is one of

the reasons I had to come here. The other is to—oh my goodness, the letter." She launched out of the water, flung the drying cloth around her and dug into her skirt pocket. She clutched the letter to her chest. "I wrote this letter for my parents, one I need them to receive in the future. They perish in a terrible fire in the year two-thousand and eleven, but they might not if they get this."

"Wheesht! The year two-thousand and eleven? Annie, now you've gone too far." She tut-tutted as she crossed to the trunk, lifted the lid and plucked out a nightrail.

"I can see you don't believe me. I tried to convince Alex of what had happened, and I was making some leeway, but he—"

"Goodness, I'm surprised your handfast husband didnae have you thrown into the dungeons for such talk. Indulging in a yarn is one thing, but believing in it is quite another." She yanked off the cloth and tugged the shift over her head. "You clearly need rest. You're home now, and you've naught to worry about."

Great. She trudged to the bed, heaved the draperies aside and climbed in. If she heard such ramblings, she probably wouldn't deem them true either. Still, she gripped Margaret's hand and pressed her point again. "I have no idea how long I'll be here. Annie disappeared within minutes of us meeting. I fear I could go as quickly. Please, promise me you'll keep this letter safe, that you'll ensure it stays here for each future chief to pass along from one to the other, then I'll know I've done all I can."

"I can see this worries you." Margaret squeezed her fingers. "If you halt this tale of time travel then I'll give you my promise to keep your letter safe."

"Absolutely. I'll not whisper a word again." Her heart lightened. She could do that, as long as her parents were given a fighting chance in the future.

"Good, because if Rory hears what you've told me, he'll believe MacDonald at fault for your madness and hunt the man down. We may have fairy blood, but we cannae travel across time. Pass me the letter. I'll keep it safe within Rory's locked library box." She handed it to her, and Margaret eyed the address she'd written on the front. "New Zealand? Where's that?"

"The other side of the world, a country as yet undiscovered."

"Annie." Aghast, she wagged a finger. "I shouldnae have asked. Will you keep your word?"

"Yes, no more talk of time travel. You've got—"

A knock sounded.

"I'll get it." She opened the door then allowed the lads and maids from earlier to clear everything away. Once they were done, Margaret returned to her side, kissed her cheek. "This letter must remain our secret. Sleep well. I'll see you in the morn." She closed the door as she left.

Gosh, had she done enough to ensure her parents' survival?

Rolling to her side, she burrowed into the soft down mattress. She edged the thick curtain aside to allow the heat from the fire through. A nice warm cocoon. Annie had not left Dunscaith and returned here. She had certainly disappeared, but to where?

Would she have long left here in the past? A day? A week? A lifetime? And what of Alex?

She wasn't done with him yet.

* * * *

Alex's men rowed through the dark, sending their birlinn swiftly across the loch toward the MacLeod stronghold. The long sea crossing was almost at an end. He'd followed closely in Rory MacLeod's wake with Mother on board, and MacLeod would be forced to honor his invitation, the Highland code of hospitality one he now counted on. Soon he'd see Anne. She'd broken her vow with him, although had MacLeod not taken her, it wouldn't have happened.

Aye, he needed more time with her. A year was what he'd

promised Anne, and a year was what he wanted.

"Dunvegan lies directly ahead." Alan eased onto the bench seat beside him. "I cannae believe we've no' seen any sign of James during our journey. He sailed days ahead of us."

"Aye, but with MacLeod turning up on our lands afore he could have arrived here, they may have passed each other at sea. We'll find him." He glared at his man. "I have no' yet forgiven you."

"I noticed."

"Go sit with my mother and guard her with your life. Upon sighting us, who knows how MacLeod will react."

"He'll no' expect us this soon, if at all."

Ahead at the edge of the sea-gate, a warning shout hailed from one guardsman to another, echoed up the winding stairs to the warriors above. They must have seen their MacDonald flag flying.

"We have yet to get past their welcoming party." He strode to the front of the birlinn and called out, "We've come at the Chief of MacLeod's invitation. I've brought Mary MacDonald."

Four of MacLeod's men waded into the water and gripped the sides of their boat. The head man's penetrating gaze drilled into him. "Ye'll need to await confirmation from my chief before being permitted on our land."

MacLeod stormed down the winding stairs. "Alex MacDonald," he boomed, his eyes glinting in the moonlight. "I've seen enough MacDonalds lately to last me a lifetime."

Alex grasped the edge of the birlinn and heaved himself into the water. Surging through it, he slogged toward MacLeod. "I handfasted with Anne as agreed and now our feud is done. I sent my brother, James, to inform you."

"I've no' seen your kin." His gaze slid over the occupants in the birlinn. "I cannae believe you brought your mother."

"After the way you stole my wife away, she wished to assure herself Anne was well. As do I."

Fists clenched, MacLeod huffed. "Annie repudiated your handfast when she agreed to return with me."

"She may have, but I still honor the vow I spoke."

"The agreement no longer stands."

He hadn't expected MacLeod to relent, but then neither would he. "My mother is cold. She does no' travel well, and this has been a difficult voyage. You did invite her."

"I didnae think you'd allow such a trip."

"She was insistent." Surely MacLeod would grant them entry. Mother was the key.

"Damn it." MacLeod stared him down. "Annie will wish to see her. If I allow it then it's with the understanding your visit here will be short. You'll no' get Annie back."

This was not the time to argue, and he had no intention of continuing their feud when he'd been set the task to end it. He was here. 'Twas the first step. "For my mother's sake, I thank you for your hospitality, no matter how short it shall be." Over his shoulder, he called to his men, "All ashore."

MacLeod's gaze narrowed, and then he bellowed instructions to his men to bring the birlinn in.

In short order they ascended the stairs and entered the keep. They were directed to the great hall, and his men offered pallets around the hearth.

MacLeod beckoned a maid forward. "Ensure Mistress MacDonald is given a comfortable chamber near Annie's, along with a bath and a meal."

"Thank you, my lord." Mary dipped her head. "'Twas a long and weary journey. I shall enjoy the kindness you offer." She followed the maid upstairs.

Highland hospitality was a sacred obligation. As MacLeod had not been able to turn them away, so must Alex respect what they'd been granted. He'd have to take great care. "I'll sleep with my men."

"Aye, as I expected. 'Tis late. We will speak in the morn, at which point you may hear from Annie her desire to remain. Following it, you will leave." MacLeod stomped away.

A score of MacLeod's warriors remained and settled in across from his men. He'd expected naught less and would have set the same precautions in place.

Near the stairwell his mother had ascended, he chose the closest pallet and stood next to it. Anne was close, asleep in one of the upper chambers. He'd come this far and now she lay just beyond his reach. Hell, he needed to see her, to ensure she was well.

"Alex." Alan clasped his shoulder. "Bide your time. Get some sleep."

He lay down in the darkened corner and pulled his plaid tight around him.

He was here. A good start.

* * * *

Tossing from side to side, Anne couldn't settle. She should be able to having ensured her parents' letter was taken care of. Alex consumed her—

A hand clamped over her mouth and she bucked against the intruder's tight hold.

She tried to kick the man who slid between the velvet curtains and rolled in beside her.

"Nay, Anne. Hold still."

A flicker of firelight tracking through the gap highlighted Alex's high cheekbones and strong jaw. She clasped his face.

"If I let go, you cannae make a sound." His gaze roamed over her. "You look well, my sweet."

She dragged him closer. Alex was here. He was real, and he'd come for her.

"Is that your agreement?"

She hooked one leg over the back of his knee and jerked him on top of her. "Mmm-hmm," she mumbled, then pried his fingers away. "I can't believe you're here."

"I couldnae stay away. I needed to hear your repudiation from your own lips."

"My vow stands firm."

"Then you shouldnae have left Dunscaith. To get you back will require a fight."

"I had to deliver my letter. That's why I left with Rory. I gave it to Margaret, and she promised to keep it safe."

"She believes you?"

"No, she thinks I'm Annie. She even insisted I not speak of my time travel and coming from the future, but it's true all the same. Do you believe me yet, Alex?"

"Nay, and in time your head will clear and you'll see the truth. Something happened for you to leave your home and travel to me but 'twas no' time travel. Mayhap you hit your head and 'tis the reason for this fantasy you weave."

"Ahh, I see. Hit my head. Of course, and to do that I might have fallen from my horse while out riding. Oh yes, and then I recalled the need to handfast with you and set straight out for Dunscaith because that had become my greatest priority. Why did I not see that?" She rubbed her nose to his. Regardless of his disbelief, she couldn't be more grateful he was here. "That would make sense, my last coherent thought being to risk my life to cross the isle and reach you. A man I'd never met before and didn't wish to handfast with. Yes, you're onto something."

"You're an imp." He swatted her backside. "I've missed your teasing ways."

"I hope you've missed more than that. But hey, you're the one who thinks I'm suffering a head injury. I'm just pointing out the reasons how that can be, or can't be. Maybe I'm even hallucinating this very second. I mean, you're in my bed, which means a MacDonald has somehow infiltrated these castle walls."

"You're no' hallucinating. Mother secured an invitation and I brought her. MacLeod had no choice but to extend his hospitality to me." His lips slowly lifted. "So I'm enjoying said hospitality, in your bed."

"Did you bolt the door?"

"Aye, but I still snuck in and could easily be found. I cannae stay."

She stroked his sides and cupped his butt. "Your place is with me."

"My place is to protect you. To see to your safety and wellbeing."

"This time period really sucks. Where I come from, provided a woman wishes it, her man can sneak into her bed without these kinds of issues. I could protect you if they came. Pass me your sword."

"Anne, you must cease all talk of—"

"Pass me your other weapon then." She wriggled against him and his cock rose and stabbed her in the belly. "Ahh, there we are. Come sheath that blade in me."

He chuckled then captured her mouth with his. He kissed her, deeply, like a man on a mission, an undertaking she didn't want him to end. He gripped her waist, his hands spanning upward, so close to her breasts.

She melted into the sheets. "Don't leave me."

"I will fight for you." He trailed kisses along her jaw and down her neck.

She arched in the hope he'd go lower. "Have you ever heard the saying, 'make love not war?'"

"Nay, but never have I heard a more fanciful wish." He swept his tongue over the rise of her breasts.

"I'm wearing too many clothes, and so are you."

"Aye, I couldnae agree more." He brushed her breasts through her nightrail. "I've heard your declaration that you wish to stay with me. That's all I need. We'll speak in the morn and present a united front before MacLeod. It'll be our first avenue of attack. I must go." Head dipped, he captured her nipple through the cotton and sucked hard.

"Alex." Fire raced through her blood. "You can't do that if you're going to go."

He released her breast, grinned then dropped a kiss on her lips. "I can and did. Sleep well, my sweet." He snuck out of her bed and crept to the door, adjusting his trews as he did.

Shoving the curtains back, she whispered, "Whatever you need me to do, I'll do it. Be careful. Don't let anyone see you."

He held a finger to his lips. "Shh, on the morrow. Goodnight."

She bit her tongue to ensure she remained quiet as he slipped out the door and closed it without a snick.

Rubbing her chest, she ached for him to return. Alex had come for her and she wanted nothing more than to be with him. "I won't leave you again, Alex. I promise you that." She wanted her parents alive and her Highland lover. Only how could she achieve that means?

She would make sure she didn't leave his side again. She'd come to Scotland to find her roots, to see where her ancestors had come from. Even though she'd never expected to find Alex, he was a man she wanted to belong to, in every sense of the word. Without a doubt Annie had made her wish to leave the past, but in doing so, had granted Anne her greatest desire.

She lifted her face to the velvet canopy. "I wish upon the Fairy Flag hidden somewhere here within Dunvegan, that my parents survive the terrible fire which took them. Allow Annie to travel through time as she wishes, but please, do not take me from Alex, not now I've found him."

All around lights shimmered, as if the stars had escaped the sky and blazed above. A mist rose and surrounded her. The stars blinked out.

"No." She clutched her belly as it rolled. "No!"

Her scream echoed through the dense fog, reverberating in her own ears.

Chapter 7

This couldn't be happening. Alex had just arrived and she hadn't had enough time with him. Thunder boomed and a cold wind whipped her nightrail against her legs. What had she been thinking to make that wish? Yes she wanted her parents alive but—

In the darkness hands grabbed her. "Anne, hold still, or you'll topple us both off this ledge."

Her feet swayed in midair. "Donald? Where did you come from?"

"I haven't left. Don't fight me." Breath heaving, the tour guide yanked her up from the abyss and onto the thin ledge beside him. "Damn, that was close. Are you hurt? Hell, where are your clothes?"

The wind beat against her. "I—I—"

"Here, take my coat." He whipped it off and wrapped it around her. "Why'd you try to jump?"

"I didn't. James pulled me through."

"Who?"

"The man who ran out of the castle." She clutched his shirtfront. "Alex rode in on his horse and the men spoke as if from centuries in the past."

"Yes, but they disappeared as you jumped." He flattened his hand against her forehead. "You feel all right. Are you certain James pulled you through? To where?"

"To the past, to the year fifteen-ninety. I've been there over a week, with both your ancestors and mine."

"Unbelievable. I made a grab for you as you jumped, and I thought I'd missed then suddenly you were there again."

"Please, believe me, Donald. I've had enough of everyone thinking me delusional." She flung open the coat he'd given her and exposed her nightrail again. "See. I've been back through time. What else could explain this?"

Swirling, eerie fog enclosed them completely. "I told you strange things have happened at these ruins, events that can't be explained. We shouldn't have crossed here. This is my fault."

"You believe me?"

"Yes, look at what you're wearing."

"Someone who finally believes me. Thank you." She grasped his hands. "Although my traveling back through time would have happened no matter where I crossed. There was another Anne, one from fifteen-ninety who made a wish upon the Fairy Flag at Dunvegan. Her family call her Annie, and she traveled to the future, while I traveled to the past. I don't know where she is, but I met her there before she disappeared again. I was supposed to travel."

"I've heard old folk stories, ones told of unexplained disturbances near the ancient stones. These ruins too."

The ruins. Alex was gone and now she balanced on the edge of the stone drawbridge at the time right after she'd met him. The sea roared and the surf washed in against the rock's sheer surface below.

Water splashed her nose then her cheek. The heavens opened and rain hit in a torrent, wiping away the fog in one hard blow. On the rock, Dunscaith emerged from the dark, the castle no more. Rubble was all that remained.

She was back in the future.

"Alex." She grasped her head as it spun.

* * * *

After stealing back downstairs, Alex eased onto his pallet. Leaving Anne had his gut rolling with turmoil. He wanted to return and hold her through the night. When had she eased her way into his affections so strongly? Or when hadn't she? Aye, from the morn of their handfast, he'd not been able to keep his hands off her.

'Twas just as well she'd declared her place was with him. He'd hold her words close. She was his wife, and a year no longer seemed enough. He had to get her out of here and back to Dunscaith where he'd wed her proper and once done, MacLeod couldn't interfere. Aye, her chief wouldn't stop him for long.

He was here, and he wasn't leaving without—

An ear-piercing scream ricocheted around the hall.

"Anne!" He bellowed her name, shot upstairs and threw open her door.

From behind him his men drew their swords. He stormed to her bed, ripped open her curtains.

Nothing but the bedding tossed around.

"Where is she?" Alan gaped.

"Search the castle," one of her kinsmen yelled.

"I'll get the chief," another snapped as he tore from the room.

Alex eyed each of his men. "She has to be somewhere. Aid the MacDonalds in searching for her. We dinnae rest until my wife is found."

* * * *

"I've got you." Donald sat beside her on her hospital bed and tucked her close. "It was a bad dream is all."

"I thought I was back with Alex. That wouldn't be a bad dream." She grasped the blanket, one perfectly knit by machine, its tag stating it was one-hundred percent wool and made in

Scotland. Out the high-rise window, other cold, colorless high-rises loomed.

Below, moving cars and occasional honks signified life moved on, but not for her. Donald had brought her here, straight from the ruins ten days ago. He'd visited her each day, along with his father.

"I've got to get out of here."

"Yes, but the doctor won't release you until you can keep your food down. Time travel clearly didn't agree with you."

"I've never been sick like this in my life." She flicked the stand holding the bag that fed her much-needed nutrients. "It's like I'm living between worlds, or times, here but not here." She gripped his collar with shaky hands. "Did you find out any information on my parents?"

"Dad's researching as we—"

"I've made a breakthrough." William marched into the room. He tugged off his woolen jersey and slung it over the back of the padded chair near the window. Seated, he leaned forward, hands clasped over his knees. "I received confirmation this morning. There's no evidence of any death certificates being issued for either of your parents."

"Then where are they?" She had no way to contact them. After the fire had destroyed her childhood home, she'd purchased a small unit a few streets over, not wanting to be too far away, although not wanting to rebuild. If she could get out of here, fly home, then she could actually begin to search for them. "I have to leave, and you two have to help me escape."

"Not until the doctor releases you for travel."

"Dad's right." Donald took her hands and slowly eased them from his collar. "Look at your skin. It's almost translucent." Turning her hands over, he scrutinized them. "I've never seen anything like it before."

"The doctor took more blood this morning, and I'm washed out because she did." She squeezed his fingers. "I'm so grateful you and William have stood by me, but I've got to get out of here. My parents aren't dead. My letter must have reached them."

She'd told them of her wish, that her parents survive the terrible fire which took them. That Annie be allowed to travel through time as she wished, but also that she not be taken from Alex. She had been, although her heart was still with him. She should have made her wish more clear.

"Anne, I have the results from your blood test." Her matronly doctor strode in, one hand clamped on a stethoscope dangling around her neck. She crossed and perched beside her. "The results are conclusive."

"Is it bad?" A shiver chased down her spine. Don't let it be bad. She had to get out of here.

"I know you took precautions against pregnancy a few years ago, but you're pregnant all the same."

Oh, and she'd told Alex that couldn't happen Wow, she was pregnant. Sure, she may not have wished for it, but since she didn't have the man, having a part of him like this was a dream.

"Your morning sickness is rather severe, and began quite quickly. We'll need to continue treatment until you show some signs of improvement." Dr. MacKinnon patted her arm. "You have particularly low iron levels, and I want you to begin taking some supplements. Once your levels are up and you're able to eat then I'll look at discharging you." She rose to her feet, dug into her pocket and removed a bottle. "At least we finally have the answer for your illness. I want you to start taking these tablets immediately."

She gripped the plastic container and nodded at the doctor. "Thank you."

"You're welcome. Try and get some rest, and if you have any questions, we'll chat on my next round." She strode out the door.

"Here's some water." William passed her a glass from the

side table.

She swallowed the meds then dropped the bottle into the pocket of her fleecy pink pajamas. Donald had brought her luggage when she'd been admitted. He'd even paid her hotel bill. She owed both him and William more than she could ever repay.

She rose and lugged her IV stand toward her drawers. She pulled out her travel documents, including her passport. "We have to get serious on finding my missing parents since I'm trapped in this room for who knows how long."

"At least there's no record of their deaths," Donald stated. "That's a start, although I wish you had some living relatives Dad and I could call. It'd make things so much easier."

"Sorry, I'm it." She passed him her travel pack. "Could you two take this to the New Zealand Embassy and explain I'm in hospital. See if they'll seek the information we need regarding my parents' current whereabouts now we know they're alive."

He flicked through her documents. "This'll help open some doors. Hold on. If your parents are alive, I wonder if your childhood home still burnt to the ground?"

Shoot. She could kick herself for not thinking of that.

"If your parents live," Donald continued, "maybe that's where they are. What's your old address and phone number?"

"We lived on 484 Ocean Beach Road in Mount Maunganui."

William nabbed a pen from his shirt pocket "Right, what was the phone number?"

Her sight dimmed and William's words were lost to her. She swayed and crumpled to the ground.

* * * *

Her head pounded as if horses stampeded within.

Oh, so not good. William. He'd wanted her phone number. She had to give that to him.

She scrubbed her head, and the drip attached at her wrist caught around her fingers. "Ow. Ow. Ow. Stupid—"

"Stay still, Annie. I dinnae know what this contraption attached to you is, but 'tis embedded in with a needle. What have you done to yourself?"

"What?" She flung her eyes open. Great, now she truly was hallucinating. "Margaret?"

"You've been missing for nigh on ten hours. The whole clan searches for you, but I cannae let them know I've found you like this. You appeared out of nowhere, right afore my eyes. You're truly no' Annie are you?"

She pushed herself upright, taking care not to bump the drip again. "I haven't been gone ten days?"

"Nay. Wait a moment." She grabbed her burgundy skirts and rushed to the door, closed it and slid the bolt into place. "What is this metal box, the rod and bag of...well, how did you get it here? Where did you go?" Margaret plucked at her fleecy pajama bottoms. "You're even wearing men's trews, pink ones. I've never seen such a sight."

Oh, she really had returned to the past. And drat, she'd left her parents behind before she'd had a chance to find them. Nothing was going her way. Except Alex was here. Her heartbeat raced. Alex was here. "Ignore the pants. My parents are alive."

"Then you traveled back to the future? Where's Annie?"

"You finally believe me?"

"Aye, it's hard no' to since you disappeared for so long and without one guard seeing you leave, and now you return out of nowhere, dressed like this, with that thing attached to you." She grasped her hands with shaky fingers. "Who would try to harm you like this? And why with such a strange contraption?"

"It doesn't hurt, or at least it didn't until I knocked it. I was sick and—" She eyed the near empty bag. "I'm going to have to take this needle out. I can't have anyone seeing it, other than Alex of course. He so needs to see this."

"We'll hide it all under your bed for now. You said ten

days? Where's my cousin?"

"I have no idea where Annie is, but my parents are no longer dead. The letter you kept for me made it to them, only I couldn't find them. They're alive, but I have no idea where in my time."

"And Annie is still living there?" Margaret fluttered her hand in front of her pale face.

"Sit." She tugged Margaret onto the bed beside her. "When you're ready, press down on this needle while I pull the tape off. You may not faint until after you've aided me."

Tears trailed down Margaret's cheeks as she pressed where she'd asked. "My cousin is living in the future. I cannae believe it. I might never see her again."

"Or you might. I have no idea how this time travel thing works. I can only say she traveled back here once, that first night I arrived at Dunscaith, and now I've traveled back and forth too. If it happened once, it could happen again."

She peeled the tape from the needle then slowly withdrew it. She wiped away the dot of blood. "Margaret, I'm pregnant. This device gave me nutrients. I've been terribly sick for the past ten days."

"Pregnant?" Margaret's face washed completely out. "You're having Alex MacDonald's bairn? But Rory willnae— oh, this is all a terrible mess."

"I need your help, but first"—she bundled up the tubing and jammed it under the bed with the stand—"I need to get dressed."

"Aye, dressed, before a guardsman returns to check this floor. I willnae fail you now." Margaret dashed to the trunk and foraged through it. "You cannae tell Rory about the bairn you carry. He'll question how it could have happened so soon and you cannae speak of those ten days."

"No problem." She dug the pills out of her pocket then stripped off her pajamas. "Having lost my family, I know exactly how important our closest are. I never thought I'd see Alex again, and now I'm back."

"Arms up." Margaret eased a day ruby-red dress over her head. The layers slid down her body and skimmed her ankles. Margaret nabbed the white ribbons dangling at her waist and laced up the front stays. She pulled the fabric snug and tied the bow along the low square neckline. "Let's tidy your hair."

She pocketed her pills and sat near the side table. "I'm so glad I met you, Margaret."

"You're a MacLeod, and kin. I'll always stand by your side, whether you're my cousin or no'." She brushed her hair.

"I haven't had family in a long time. Now I do."

"You also have a man who cares for you. We all heard your scream and when I raced in here to find you gone, Alex was issuing orders to his men. He said he wouldnae rest until his wife was found, and he surely meant it. At dawn both my clansmen and his began searching the forest."

Out the window, the sun was high. It was past midday. "When will he be back?"

"Once he finds you." Margaret braided her hair and secured it with a red ribbon. "Rory is with him. He was certain Alex had something to do with your disappearance and didnae care to let him out of his sight."

"Alex will be beside himself."

"It appeared so." Margaret gripped her shoulders. "What happened to you must stay between us. I believe because I saw you appear out of thin air. I know what you speak of is true, but no other will see it that way. I have to protect both you and my cousin should Annie return."

A knock sounded on the door and Margaret called out, "Who is it?"

"Mary MacDonald. Has there been any word on Anne?"

"Just a moment, Mary." Margaret held a finger to her lips. "She's been so worried about you. We'll say you walked in your sleep and I found you in my dressing room, that I didnae think to look there."

"Absolutely. I must go to her." She raced to the door and flung it open.

"Oh my, am I seeing things?" Mary staggered back. "Anne?"

"It's me." She pulled Mary into her arms. "I'm so sorry to have caused such an uproar. I've missed you."

"Where have you been?" She caught Anne's face between her hands, her gaze searching hers. "Last eve, I heard your scream. Were you hurt?"

"No, but I woke a little while ago inside Margaret's dressing room. Sometimes I sleep walk."

"You look exhausted, as if you've had no sleep at all." Her gaze traveled over her body. "And thin. You've lost weight since I last saw you. Come, you should eat." She wrapped an arm around Anne's waist and guided her downstairs.

"I'll organize a meal," Margaret said from her other side. "Something simple. How does bread and honey sound?"

"Perfect." Maybe she'd be able to keep it down. Oh, she was back. This was real. Her mind was still cloudy, but clearing more with each minute that passed. She hoped William and Donald would keep searching for her parents even though she'd gone.

"I willnae be long, and I'll send one of the lads out to inform Rory you've been found." Margaret rushed off toward the kitchen.

Mary urged her to sit at the dais. "Almost everyone has joined in the search."

"I didn't mean to cause such mayhem." Gripping Mary's hand, she whispered, "I saw Alex, ah, last night before I wandered off." Great. She'd have to keep track of her days. So many lost, and her mind wasn't where it should be. She needed sustenance, badly.

"He risks so much when MacLeod has already made his

intentions clear." Mary leaned in. "We dinnae need to have hostilities rise again between our clans."

"What exactly do you mean? What's Alex done?"

"Naught yet, but his mind is set. He wants you back."

"I want him too." She longed to be with Alex, although she was living in Annie's world. "We'll have to tread carefully."

"Here we are." Margaret bustled in and set a tray before her. Steam wafted from a mug of tea, and she longed for the warmth it would provide.

"Thank you." She cupped the mug.

Margaret sat, gave her a nod. "Eat slowly."

She tore the thick slice of bread into bites and tried a bit. This had to go down. She chewed and tentatively swallowed.

Her belly revolted at the intrusion of food, but she kept her lips clamped together.

Margaret rubbed her back. "I sent another lad to the healer, asking her to come." To Mary, she said, "It must be a touch of sea-sickness. It's no' unusual for my cousin to suffer from it after such a long trip."

"Oh, you should have said, my dear. No wonder you look so pale."

"I'll come right." Or she better. Alex already worried enough without seeing her like this.

She prodded another piece of bread into her mouth then quickly washed it down with a sip of tea. This time her belly didn't heave. Okay, good.

"Look at you." Mary brushed her fingers across her cheeks. "Keep eating."

She took another bite and again kept it down.

Margaret smiled. "That's—"

"Anne MacLeod!" Rory yelled her name as he stormed into the keep. The Norse ancestry of their clan was never more obvious than right now as Rory, like a Viking of old strode toward her.

She wobbled as she rose. "I'm sorry for any trouble I've caused. Margaret found me this morning asleep in her dressing room."

"And you've only just awoken?"

"Yes, I was exhausted."

"That cannae happen again." He grasped her shoulders then dropped a kiss on the top of her head. "Do you hear me?"

"Anne!" Alex raced into the hall, his golden eyes ablaze. "You're back." He heaved her away from Rory and into his arms. "Where the hell have you been?"

"I'm so sorry." His hold, so tight, almost prevented her from taking a decent breath. "Apparently I walked in my sleep and ended up in Margaret's dressing room. I didn't mean to worry anyone."

"We've spent hours hunting for you in the woods."

"I'm truly sorry. I missed you." Arms around his waist, she gripped his shirt smeared with dirt and dried nettles.

"As I—"

"That's enough. Step away from my cousin, MacDonald." Rory shoved between them.

"You took her from me." Alex pushed back. "She's mine to care for."

"Her welfare is no longer your concern."

"A technicality, and you know it."

"Stop it. Both of you." She raced around Rory and grabbed Alex from behind. "This arguing won't solve a thing, and I"— she swayed—"I—"

Black dots danced before her eyes as the room spun, and then nothing.

Chapter 8

Alex scooped Anne into his arms as she crumpled. With his cheek near her mouth, he waited for her breath to touch his skin. A caress of air gave proof she'd fainted. The tension in his gut eased. "She breathes."

"Pass her to me," MacLeod demanded.

"Nay, I'll take her to her chamber." He marched toward the stairwell.

His mother snagged MacLeod's arm. Good. She would gain him some time. "Alex would never harm his wife. Allow him to see to her."

Margaret raced to Alex and whispered, "Anne's no' been well since she awoke. I've called a healer."

"Explain her sickness." He bounded to the second floor, kicked open her chamber door and tramped inside.

"You'll have to ask her after she awakes." Margaret shut the door and bolted it.

"Alex?"

Anne stirred in his arms, and gently, he laid her down. "I'm here, my sweet. What sickness is this you have?"

"I didn't sleep walk." Her eyes fluttered open, so big and blue. "I traveled back—I mean forward to the future, to

Dunscaith where I first came through the portal on the drawbridge. I was there for ten days and discovered my parents are alive, only I don't know where they are. I couldn't find them."

"Speak the truth, Anne. No more of this gibberish. 'Tis making you sick."

She cupped his face and smiled. "I truly was there for ten days, in hospital, suffering from morning sickness. I know I said I couldn't get pregnant, but it appears I can and did."

"You're—" He shook his head. "'Tis impossible."

"Oh come on. We both know that's entirely possible." She arched a brow. "Tell me. What will it take to convince you I've been gone ten days?"

"Naught." How could he make her see sense? Aye, a pregnancy was possible, but she couldn't know this soon. "You've been gone ten hours. Every single one has burdened my heart."

"I have never felt this sick in my entire life." She jabbed a finger into his chest. "It's been ten days, and each one has been a burden to me too." She looked at Margaret. "Grab the drip and show Alex. If he still doesn't believe me then knock him over the head with it. I'm over trying to prove I've come from the future."

Margaret scrambled to her knees, jerked the equipment from under the bed and shoved it into his hands. "Alex, Anne speaks the truth. She appeared out of thin air afore my eyes and this contraption was attached to her. What's this, if not something from the future?"

What a strange contraption. The box was sturdy and the steel well-crafted like his sword, but clearly not from this time. The rest was unlike anything he'd ever seen. He couldn't even put a name to it. "What did you need all this for, Anne?"

"It provided nutrients because I couldn't keep any food down. Those are stored as a liquid in that see-through bag. The nutrients drip down the plastic tube and through a needle directly into my body." She pointed to her punctured wrist. "It went in right here."

"She speaks the truth." Margaret backed toward the door. "I'm going to check on where the healer is. I willnae be long."

"Unbelievable." He followed her to the door and slid the bolt into place behind her. The evidence was real. He couldn't deny it.

"You finally believe me?"

"Aye, I've seen what could only come from another time." He shoved the thing under the bed then turned her hand over and examined her wrist. Someone had thrust a needle into her here. If only he could make them pay with their life. "Who did this?"

"It was done to aid me, not harm."

"It shall never happen again, just as you shall never return to the future." She carried his bairn, and the agony of her disappearance had cut into him so hard that to live without her would be akin to death.

"I don't have any control over the portal."

"You must have activated it somehow." She slowly nodded, her lips pressed together as if she didn't wish to admit what she'd done. "Speak it."

"I made a wish upon the Fairy Flag seconds before I was taken."

"Then no more wishes. Not one, Anne. I cannae lose you again."

"My parents are alive." Her eyes brightened. "I want to see them again."

"No. More. Wishes."

"I really want to see them."

"You dinnae listen, lass." He kissed her. She tasted so sweet, and damn it, he'd missed her in the worst way. She wouldn't leave his sight again. "I'll find a way to change MacLeod's decision, and if no', be prepared to leave at a moment's notice."

"You're a stubborn man, but I'm glad you're mine." She wound her arms around his neck and snuggled. "I'm sorry about the wishes, but I can't promise I won't make any more. I'm a little impulsive like that."

"You'll obey and give me your word."

"Well, you could offer some persuasion. I'd totally be up for it."

He kissed her again, plundering her mouth as he needed. Touching her, having her body pressed against his was heaven, a sensation he never wanted to give up. He yearned for her, and the bairn. So much was at stake. He must fix all that had gone wrong and get her back to Dunscaith. He spread his palm over her belly. A life they'd created beat within.

She writhed against him. "Did I tell you I missed you?"

Skin. He needed to touch her without the barrier of her clothing. He stroked her hip and down her thigh then heaved up the folds of her pretty red dress. He caressed the milky flesh of her inner thigh. Her heat pulsed, so close.

Beyond aroused, he slid a finger inside her. He rubbed her tight nub and she released a soft sigh.

"Alex, you have a magical touch and I'm about to forget where we are." Her hips moved and she pressed harder into his palm.

"Then forget, but I must remain alert." He stroked deeper until she panted for a breath.

"In that case before I do. I, Anne MacLeod, from the year two-thousand and fourteen, pledge my troth to Alexander William MacDonald. Oh." She bucked against his hand. "With his wicked touch, I take him as my husband for the next year and a day."

"Aye, and I, Alexander William MacDonald, pledge my troth to Anne MacLeod from the year two-thousand and fourteen. I give my word I shall find a way to take her as my wife, for all time, present and future."

Easing her legs further apart, he added another finger and plunged deeper to hit the spot that would make her come apart in his arms.

She arched into his touch, urged him for more. "Alex, kiss me, please."

He seized her mouth, kissing her with all the longing that ruled his heart. Desire drove him as her heartbeat thumped against his chest and below, her channel tightened wickedly around him.

She moaned as he kissed her, and then with his fingers alone, he drove her over the edge.

Aye, he desired all of her, and not for a year and day. Forever wouldn't be long enough. "I'll never leave you. I give you my word."

* * * *

After the orgasm from heaven, Anne held Alex's last words close to her heart. "I know you'll never leave me. Right from the beginning, I sensed you never would. Somehow and someway."

"Aye, you did. I heard you whisper those words in your sleep that first night." He kissed her belly then drew her skirts down and tucked them under her legs. "You said your parents are alive."

"Yes, and it's about time you believed me." She rolled toward him.

"Time travel knows no bounds. You were gone ten days instead of ten hours. Tell me exactly what you and Annie spoke of when you first met at Dunscaith."

"I gave her my name, and she asked if I had any kin who'd miss me. I told her no, that my parents had passed away three years ago. They were lost to me when our house burnt down. She promised me she'd fix what she'd started. I don't think she truly intended for me to end up at Dunscaith, or at least that's the impression she gave me." She scrambled into a sitting position then peeked past the bed curtains to the door. "Is it safe for you to still be here?"

"Mother waylaid MacLeod, and dinnae worry over me." He planted his booted feet on the floor. "I can hold my own against Rory MacLeod."

"I'm sure you can, but I prefer not to cause more trouble than what's necessary." She stroked his muscular arm under the warmth of his linen shirt. So strong, and all hers.

"You've been trouble since the moment I laid eyes on you." He caught her hand and pressed it flat to his chest. "And I wouldnae change a thing. Is there aught more you've neglected to tell me?"

"Neglected?" She smacked him. "That's not even remotely funny."

"Never withhold from me again, whether I wish to listen or no'." He kissed her, so tenderly she melted back against him. "I want to see your body grow ripe with my bairn. Do you understand?"

"Yes." She touched her nose to his. "I want lots of—" Her stomach rolled and her sight dimmed. She fought the bile rising in her throat as Alex became a mere dot. She reached for him, but he'd vanished. Please, no.

The dark void spun her away.

* * * *

"Damn it, nay." Anne shimmered and faded before Alex's eyes. He tried to grab her, but from one second to the next, she was gone. He slammed his fist into the wall. She hadn't made another wish, and she'd been back for such a short time.

"Alex."

A rap sounded.

"'Tis Margaret. The healer's in the village and willnae return until nightfall. How's Anne?"

He flung open the door and ushered her in. "Gone. She disappeared, back to the future. I couldnae keep her with me."

"What should we do? Rory instructed me to watch over her and send you down."

Hell. He paced the room. Why had time taken her away again?

"You'll have to go. I've never seen my brother so impatient."

"Afore I do, I need to write Anne, and then we'll do what we must until she returns." He'd not accept any other outcome, but to have her by his side.

Searching the corner desk, he found paper and ink. Scrawling across the thick parchment, he wrote to the woman who held his heart, to do everything she could to return to him. He wouldn't allow her to raise their bairn alone, and he'd be waiting for her, always and forever. It was a message she'd better damn well receive. Once done, he folded the paper, sealed it and handed it to Margaret. "Ensure this remains with the missive Anne wrote for her parents."

"I've stored her letter in the library's safe box. I'll add it straight away."

"Thank you. I'll never forget your aid. Anne must return, and the moment she does, come and get me." She would return to him.

"Of course."

He closed Anne's door, and his Mother walked toward him from the stairwell. She tugged him into a darkened recess to the side of the passageway. "I spoke to MacLeod at length of Anne's time with us, of how much she enjoyed herself. He was insistent those memories would serve her well after we left, that it should be a fine day for sailing on the morrow. I can fake an illness if you wish."

"Do it. Though I'm no' sure how long your sickness will need to be."

"'Twill last as long as you say. I feel a deep chill in my bones." She kissed his cheek then strode to her chamber.

He marched down the winding stairs. The precious time he'd shared with Anne had taught him a great deal. Because of a wish both she and her ancestor had made on the MacLeod's Fairy Flag, she'd traveled through time, and not only once. She would come back to him, and if she didn't, he would move heaven and earth to get to her. Mayhap that damn flag was the key?

Where did MacLeod keep his famed talisman? 'Twas said the magical flag had been the means to which the MacLeod clan had defeated his own clan once, although that battle had been well before his time. First though, he had to deal with MacLeod. The man was known for his incredible strength, of both body and mind, but 'twas the latter he had to sway.

In the great hall, he searched the dimmed interior. Six MacLeod men stood stationed around the hall. Alan waited at the side, speaking with James.

He marched toward them, clasped his brother's shoulder. "Finally you show yourself. We did no' pass you at sea."

"Alex." James's expression was grave as he pulled him close. "I've been waiting in the village for word of the MacLeod chief's return. Alan told me Anne is here."

"Aye." He lowered his voice as James had done. "Mother's unwell. We'll stay until she's able to travel, and once she is, we take Anne with us."

"I heard she repudiated the handfast."

"It was no' her intention."

"Then what do you propose to do about MacLeod? Let's no' forget there's only one exit, and by a well-guarded sea-gate at that."

"My vow to her remains firm. First, I'll speak to MacLeod and attempt to sway his mind."

"He awaits you in the side room." He motioned toward it. "Would you like some company?"

"Nay, I'll deal with MacLeod, but I have a request of you

and Alan. Find out what you can about the Fairy Flag."

"Shall do."

"My thanks." He entered the lion's den. 'Twas a small dining room with a narrow window overlooking the inner courtyard. Outside two-score of MacLeod warriors, outfitted for training, had assembled. Another score watched from the sidelines.

MacLeod stoked the fire. "Take a seat, MacDonald." He tossed the stick into the flames and rose. "We need to talk."

On the table, a rolled parchment tied with black ribbon looked all too familiar. 'Twas his agreement. He had an exact copy at Dunscaith. "I'm aware of what that says."

"Read it again. You need a reminder of the wording." MacLeod scraped out a chair and sat. "Go ahead, open it."

"There is naught I've forgotten." He took the seat opposite, unfurled the paper and scanned it. He and Anne had spoken their vows before the designated date. "What in particular would you like me to take note of?"

"'Tis a handfast, a temporary union should the marriage vows no' be spoken, which they haven't. And willnae." MacLeod's eyes glinted. "Why do you insist on having her back?"

"My vow still stands, and Anne never intended to break hers. Had you no' come, she wouldnae have."

"My cousin had no say over the original agreement, and she has none now it's ended."

"I want her back."

"You cannae have her."

"She carries my—" Nay, 'twas too soon for any such news in this time. "She may carry my bairn."

"If she does, 'tis hers and will be raised here. That was agreed upon in the contract should a babe be conceived. Perhaps you should take another look at what you hold."

Aye, he'd agreed to such, but then he'd never intended such

intimacies between him and Anne. He wouldn't stand down on his decision. "The short time I've been with Anne has no' been long enough for tensions between our clans to diffuse."

"Those tensions arose because of your chief. He's no longer around, nor will he be for some time to come."

"Having her at Dunscaith is a solid reminder we no longer fight."

"We fight now. A better reminder would be if you left."

"I will, with her by my side."

"She stays."

"We will speak our vows again. I demand it."

MacLeod shoved his chair back and marched to the door. "There will be no vows spoken. I willnae sway from my decision." He instructed his men to remain on guard.

The warning was clear. Anne wouldn't be permitted to leave Dunvegan.

Chapter 9

Anne clutched the back of the padded chair to regain her balance after the jump through time. The rich burgundy fabric, highlighted by the moonlight streaming through the window was all too familiar. She patted her scratched up desktop. Solid wood. In the corner her childhood bed sat. Nothing had been destroyed. She flicked on the light. The ashes of her home hadn't fluttered away in the breeze. "I'm home. I'm really home."

Footsteps pounded down the hallway. Annie raced into the room, her white-gold hair breezing over her shoulders. "Oh my goodness. You're here."

"This is where you ended up?"

"Aye, welcome home." Dressed in yellow brushed cotton pajamas, she crossed the room and grasped her hands. "I'm sorry we parted last time so quickly."

"Me too. What year have I arrived in?"

"Two-thousand and fourteen. After I left you at Dunscaith, I came through the portal and landed in your apartment a few streets over. The strangest thing happened. Your parents arrived on your doorstep after receiving your new address from the police, only instead of you, they got me. They told me as soon as they'd disposed of the heater, it was suddenly two-thousand and fourteen. Three years had passed and the letter you'd sent them was still on the table, opened as they'd left it. I believe my arrival here triggered whatever was needed to move them back fully into time."

"What happened next?"

"They brought me here and together we tried to sort out what to do. Though we didnae speak again to the police. Fairy magic was clearly at work." She wrung her hands together. "I'm so sorry. For days we considered every single angle and 'twas only once we received a call from Scotland that we had something to work on. Your parents left immediately."

"What call?"

"One from Donald and William MacDonald. They told us they knew where you were, or at least they did. You'd just been sucked back through a portal afore their eyes. Your parents have gone to Scotland."

"But I only left Donald and William a few hours—" Oh, stupid damn time travel. "When did Donald and William call?"

"'Tis been six days since they spoke through that strange device which captured their voices. Time has no meaning until we've arrived." She pulled her into a hug. "Your parents are wonderful. Your letter to them was very clear. They cannae wait to see you."

"Ha, that would be nice," she mumbled into Annie's pajama top, no, one of her old pajama tops. "How come you didn't go with them?"

"I've no passport, and even though I could use yours since we're identical, Donald and William had it."

"Argh, that means we're both stuck here."

"I don't mind. I love your country. The beach is beyond your window, and the sand is so soft, the water such a clear blue. 'Tis no wonder MacLeods traveled halfway across the world to settle here."

"Alex needs me. We handfasted, and then Rory came for

me, you, I mean—well, you know what I mean. He came and I returned with him to Dunvegan. That's where I made a wish upon the Fairy Flag as well."

"You did? 'Tis the power behind our travel. What was your wish?"

"That my parents survive the terrible fire which took them. To allow you to travel through time as you wished, but that I not be taken from Alex."

"With our wishes made, our travel may be intertwined. You have come to me, once at Dunscaith and now here."

"Yes, but I need to see my parents, and I also need to get back to Alex. He followed me to Dunvegan. You wouldn't believe how stubborn he is."

"You've come to care for him?"

"More than anything." She palmed her chest. "My heart aches for him, and I carry his child. He knows, and I'm sure right now he's peeved I disappeared the way I did."

"A bairn." She hugged her. "Goodness, our Highland men are incredibly obstinate, although I don't know how you'll get back to him. The portal has a mind of its own."

She swayed on her feet. "Sorry, it's been a long day."

"Dinnae apologize to me. Come. I'll see to your care." She guided her out the door and down the cream carpeted hallway.

Colorful prints of her family graced the sea-blue walls, a montage from over the years. Her favorite was one of the three of them sitting at the base of the sand dunes. The foamy waves had rolled in and tickled their toes. Memories surged. "After the fire, I had nothing, not one of these prints. Now, it's all back. Amazing."

"You have a wonderful family." Annie led her across the kitchen to the side alcove.

"I've missed this place." Silver-edged blue curtains adorned the bay windows and she sat underneath them on the padded seat. She stroked the covers sewn in the same luscious fabric. On the kitchen countertop, Mum's glorious white roses bloomed in a sparkling crystal vase. "Did you pick those?"

"Aye, they're beautiful. Morainne's rose garden is stunning." Annie nabbed a credit card from the bench then sat beside her. "She gave me this and a number which unlocks money from those machines which hand it out. I had some practice before she and Tor left, but 'tis good you're here to aid me."

"I'm so sorry." How could she have forgotten how scary the future must seem to Annie. Sure, her ancestor had made the wish, which had started it all, but she was also here, trying to fix what she'd begun. "I met Margaret. She insisted we not tell Rory what had happened, that he'd never believe and only blame Alex for my loss of mind."

"Aye, she's right. It would take a miracle for Rory to believe you were no' me. Look at us. We're the same, even down to the tiny mole we have above our left eyebrow. We must be close in age"

"My birthday is June first. I'm twenty-one."

Those identical eyebrows rose. "I too am one and twenty, June first. Blood of my blood." Annie clasped her hands. "That could be another reason our wish was granted."

"What happened to your parents? I've heard they passed away, but not how."

Tears welled in Annie's eyes. "They should never have died. Three years past we were traveling to Edinburgh. Mother and I sat in the cart as Father and several of our guardsmen rode with us. Such rugged terrain, but still we traveled the roads instead of the waterways. One of the wheels came loose and we had to stop. The moment we did, a savage party of ruffians stormed out of the forest. They wielded two claymores each and attacked with ferocity."

"Why?" Oh, poor Annie. She must have been terrified.

"There is such unrest in the Highlands. The king wishes the

wealth of Skye for himself and if a clan denies what he requests, they soon find disfavor and bounties on their heads. A number of clans have lost their lands. Those cast out take what they can, where they can. 'Tis a game of survival, although many are strong, highly trained warriors. This band of ruffians was one such group."

"But you survived."

"Father tossed me his dirk and told me to take Mother and run. She wouldnae leave him, and I couldnae drag her away. Father died protecting the two of us."

"And your mother?" She wiped her wet cheeks.

"We were taken. Mother fought her captor and hit her head on a low tree branch as we passed underneath it. She never recovered from the blow."

"What about you?"

"I was dumped in the middle of their encampment and held as a hostage. The leader sent word to Rory."

"You were held for ransom?"

"Aye, but Rory planned his own attack against the thugs. He tortured the messenger until he broke. 'Twas only five days after my parents' death when Rory stormed into camp. I've never seen him so as I did that day. He went berserk, killing every single man who'd attacked us. Not one man was granted leniency. 'Twas a message well sent, that none would ever attack his clan so again."

"I'm sorry." She hugged Annie as fresh tears rolled down her cheeks.

"Some time has passed and my heart is less burdened. The good memories have risen to override the bad. I keep the precious times with my loved ones close."

"What happened next?"

"Rory took me in after my parents' death, and though he is a chief and a warrior first, I have been privileged to have been in his care. You said he came for me—I mean you."

"Yes. The Chief of MacDonald was captured by the king's men."

"Oh." Annie rubbed her chin. "With Donald MacDonald out of the way, there would be no need for the handfast."

"Exactly, but I'd already spoken my vows, only I broke them when I left with Rory to ensure my letter made it to my parents."

"Rory would use such a thing to his advantage. Hmm, what to do. I must think on it." She wandered into Mum's cozy kitchen. From the crockery cupboard, she nabbed two glasses and set them on the sand-colored countertop. "Juice of the orange, or milk?"

"Orange juice."

She took the milk from the fridge, poured two glasses then passed her one. "Milk is better for the bairn. Would you like a sandwich?"

"No, I just—"

"Food is good for the bairn too." Annie removed four slices of bread from the bag and laid them on a wooden board.

"Okay, I should be trying to up my iron levels anyway. Toss some meat on that if there's some, and I'll try and keep it down."

"Morning sickness?" Annie buttered two slices, fetched some sliced ham from the fridge and slapped the sandwich together. Passing her the meal on a plate, she added, "Is there aught I can do to help?"

"I don't think so. I feel all right at the moment. I'll eat this slowly." She nibbled on the sandwich.

"I have a thought." Annie lathered honey on her sandwich, cut it in half then returned and sat beside her. "The handfast was to take place afore the first of the coming month."

"Yes, it did."

Annie smiled, rather slyly. "Ah, but who's to say it can't take place twice?"

"Rory no doubt, and if you haven't noticed, look where I

am."

"Aye, that is one problem, or mayhap two."

"I also need to consider my parents."

"Ah, or mayhap three. Still, enough of that." Annie tapped Anne's knee. "Worry willnae get us anywhere. I said I'd sort this, and somehow I will."

Three problems, and a distance of over four-hundred years spanning them.

Great. Annie fixing this was something she'd like to see.

* * * *

Alex paced Anne's chamber. "She will return."

"It's been two days." Margaret perched on the end of the bed, wringing her hands in the lilac folds of her gown. "What if she does no' come back? Annie still hasn't."

That hadn't passed his notice. His first intended bride hadn't been seen again since Anne had arrived. He halted at the window, gripped the stone sill. The loch remained calm with nary a ripple. Its glassy surface was at great counter to the storm of emotions roiling within him. "Anne will come back. I will hunt her down if she does no'."

"Rory grows restless. He continues to ask about her, and I cannae keep him from this chamber for much longer."

Margaret had informed MacLeod Anne had the same chest sickness as Mary, both suffering terribly from their travel across the sea.

"Continue to keep the door barred. Do whatever you can to keep him from entering." Below in the inner courtyard both his warriors and MacLeod's men trained, each clan keeping to their side. "I need to join my men."

"Go. I'll send word if she returns."

Anne would come back to him. He wouldn't accept anything else.

'Twas a mantra he recited over and over as he left Margaret behind and stormed outside.

At the edge of the courtyard, he eyed the Fairy Tower. 'Twas where Rory MacLeod's chamber was located, not in the old keep where he'd just been.

The front door of the tower opened and MacLeod stepped out in his great plaid belted at his waist. Their gazes clashed, and MacLeod tipped his chin up then stared him down. "Do you wish to train, MacDonald?"

From the sheath across his back, Alex slid his claymore free and held it aloft. He wanted nothing more than to release this tension tying his muscles in knots. "I thought you'd never ask."

MacLeod withdrew his own sword and advanced. "To the first who yields goes defeat."

"Aye, that shall be you." Alex strode into the center of the yard.

Cheers sounded from his men and MacLeod's. They formed a solid circle around them.

Alex eyed MacLeod's stance as he softened his footing in preparation to attack.

They circled each other, MacLeod matching him in height and breadth. Good. An even match. He enjoyed nothing more than battling an adversary such as this. "When you're—"

"I'm always ready, MacDonald." MacLeod struck and Alex blocked. Their weapons clashed dead center, steel ringing loud against steel. "Best you never forget that."

"Then dinnae hold back on my account." He came at MacLeod, landed several hard blows one after the other.

"You favor your right." MacLeod twirled then attacked on his left, each hit stronger than the last.

He would fight, for Anne, for him, for their future together. Rory MacLeod would be the first to yield, because he never would. "Aye, but I can bide my time until you tire with such play."

MacLeod grunted. "Strong words."

"More like accurate." Alex switched their positions. He

sprang forward and caught MacLeod on his left. Battle lust rode him hard. The itch to kill throbbed through his blood. "Let's battle."

"You're an admirable opponent, MacDonald." MacLeod's gaze flashed with determination. "But I'm bred from Vikings. We never concede defeat."

"You will this day."

"Alex!" Margaret raced out the door of the keep. "Mary has asked for you. 'Tis urgent."

He swung his claymore down on MacLeod's blade, every muscle in his body on fire with rage. Mother no doubt watched from her window. "Tell her I'll be up shortly."

Margaret stood at the edge of the circle, one hand pressed to her chest. "I'll tell her no such thing. Rory, this fight must end. The MacDonalds are our guests."

MacLeod smirked at his sister. "'Tis no' a fight. We are enjoying the sunshine and fresh air while partaking in exercise."

"Dinnae you try to wheedle your way out of this." She ran to the central well, heaved up a bucket of water then marched toward them.

"Lass, dinnae even think—"

She tossed cold water at them, and it washed away the fury that had consumed Alex.

MacLeod slipped then righted himself with a chuckle. "Sister, that was wasteful."

She stepped between them, eyeing her brother. "No more of your training. 'Tis getting late and the kitchen staff stand ogling you two instead of tending to this eve's meal. You may train again in the morn."

MacLeod leaned in and tweaked Margaret's nose. "Aye, you may have your way this one time."

Alex dipped his head respectfully toward Margaret. "Excuse me while I go and see my mother."

"Thank you." Huffing, she planted her hands on her hips.

"Sorry to have wet you. Mary will greatly appreciate your visit."

Sheathing his claymore, he backed away. Booming their congratulations, his men surrounded him. Had Margaret not intervened he would have won that round with MacLeod, but maybe 'twas best she had. They were guests, of which he currently needed to remain. He had to keep his head.

James gripped his shoulder. "We need to speak."

"About?" He moved out of the others' hearing range.

"While you fought, and MacLeod's men were so engrossed, Alan and I searched for the Fairy Flag. It seemed logical for MacLeod to keep his talisman close, very close."

"You searched the Fairy Tower?"

"Aye, and the old keep, but we've found naught so far. If the flag exists, 'tis kept securely hidden."

"It exists." Anne would not have been taken from him without its magic. "Continue with your search. Take every opportunity you can to find that flag."

He would get Anne back and he wouldn't rest until he did.

She was his, heart, body and soul.

For all time, not just the past.

Chapter 10

"How do those machines fly so high?" Annie gripped the railing of the glass viewing room at Auckland's international airport. "'Tis a miracle for sure when they appear so large and cumbersome."

Smiling, Anne rested her head against Annie's shoulder. Her ancestor's curiosity knew no bounds. Keeping up with her barrage of questions over the past two days had been both exhausting and comforting. Her enthusiasm for this time at least distracted her constant thoughts of Alex. "They run on fuel and with very large engines."

"Which one will Morainne and Tor be on?"

"You can't see it yet, but their plane will be here soon." Thank goodness she'd been able to reach Donald and William the morning after she'd arrived. Being able to tell them she'd traveled through time again and was now with Annie, had eased some of her worry.

Donald had passed the phone to Dad. He'd demanded she not disappear again, his voice and hers breaking as they spoke.

"I'm s-so sorry, Dad."

"I know, honey. We miss you. Don't go anywhere."

"I'll try very hard not to."

"Your mother needs to speak to you, and before she knocks me over with her excitement."

Mum had half-growled, half-sobbed down the line. "I am going to tie you down the moment I see you. I miss you. We'll head to the airport and catch the first flight home. You make sure you're waiting for us when we arrive. If you're not, you're grounded."

"I'm an adult. You haven't grounded me since I was thirteen."

"I'll start again if it's necessary. You've taken years off my life with that letter and your sudden—oh my goodness, what am I saying? You saved our lives, and we love you for it."

"Just hurry home, Mum."

"We will. We got your letter days before the fire. We had the heater in our bedroom removed then checked over. The wiring was far below grade. We didn't even know it was a hazard waiting to explode."

"I wasn't home that night. I'd gone for a sleepover at Jane's place."

"I remember that part, and as soon as we disposed of the heater, it was suddenly two-thousand and fourteen. Three years had passed and your opened letter was still on the table. We called the police and discovered you had a new address. Then we met Annie, and she told us of her wish and the two of you trading places in time. It seemed Annie's arrival here triggered whatever was needed to move us back fully into time."

"Annie told me what happened, that fairy magic must have been at work."

"Yes. The last I recalled at the time was wondering why you'd send your father and me a letter on such old parchment. It was sealed inside a courier envelope with another letter addressed to you. The paper was so brittle but it held your handwriting."

"Hold on. One addressed to me?"

"Yes, I have it with me. It has the name Alex MacDonald on the outside under yours."

"Alex never wrote me a—" Oh, unless he had right after she'd last left. "What does it say?"

"I haven't opened it, but I'll give it to you once we're home. I can't believe we've lost three years. All of them gone."

"We'll be back together soon."

"Yes, very soon."

"Hurry home, Mum. I love you."

"I love—"

"Anne, how do they make this sheet of glass so wide?" Annie tapped the massive window pane then pressed her cheek against its cool surface. "I mean look at this. I don't see any joins and 'tis so long and in one piece."

"The joins are so well flushed together you can't see them. If you step back though, you might."

"How does it no' cave in?" Her frown deepened.

"It's reinforced."

"Reinforced?" She shook her head. "Nay, I dinnae see this reinforcing."

"It's inside the glass. Its strength comes from how it's forged."

"But—"

She clasped Annie's shoulders. "We should go and check the board and make sure my parents' flight remains on time."

"Aye, we should. That device with all those red letters and numbers constantly changes without anyone's hand upon it. It has a mind of its own." They walked toward the stairs. "How does that happen? Oh, and look there, that lady is still selling chocolate. I cannae believe she has such an endless supply, or so many people wander past and no' partake of the delicacy."

"Neither can I." She giggled.

"You're making fun of me. Shame on you." Annie nabbed her hand, veered left and raced them toward the woman wearing a bright purple, ruffled fairy dress. Annie stopped and Anne bumped into her. "Miss, allow us to unburden you of bar or two of your chocolate."

"Certainly." The sales lady dipped her head.

Annie dug into the pocket of her red jeans and removed the card she called a thing of great magic. "Take what you need from here."

"Actually"—Anne looped her arm through Annie's—"we'll take four bars."

"We will?" Annie's eyes widened and she clapped. "Of course we will. Your parents must have one each too. Why didnae I think of that? My apologies." Annie paid for the chocolate.

"You're forgiven."

The flight information screen showed her parents' flight was a mere ten minutes away. She needed to see them so desperately. It had been far too long.

She rubbed her arms, wrinkling up the long sleeves of her sheer butter-yellow blouse. For the past two days, even as much as she'd longed to return to Alex, she'd longed equally to see her parents. Each morning she'd awoken and stared at the framed print she'd removed from the wall and propped beside her bed. She wanted them back now.

"Here you go." Annie passed her a bar of chocolate then frowned. "Oh dear, you look just as you did this morn, very pensive."

Annie had slept beside her in the spare bed, although they'd shoved the two beds together to make one, neither wanting any great distance between them in case the other was taken. "I'm nervous."

"Dinnae be. It's no' good for the bairn."

Anne stroked her belly. "I'm feeling much better now. I even helped you consume that last bar of chocolate, and I intend to eat the next one all on my own."

"Aye, but even should I feel ill, I could still devour a bar of chocolate. That's no' a very convincing argument." Annie tapped her nose. "How much longer until your parents arrive?"

"Soon. Come on, we'll head to arrivals." She led Annie toward the escalator.

"'Tis mesmerizing." Annie jiggled as they moved down the traveling belt. "One does no' even need to walk, and there is naught one wheel which might break."

"You should see how wonderful it is to travel in an elevator, although we'll keep that for another time. I think you've had enough excitement for the day. I know I have." She dragged Annie past another lady selling chocolate. People milled near the roped off arrival doors. She tapped her foot, the clack of her heel echoing around her.

"How long until they come through?" Annie fidgeted with the hem of her white and red striped blouse. "You're making me nervous."

"Too long." Squeezing her eyes shut, she willed her parents to hurry.

There was no time to delay.

* * * *

Pacing the rear battlements of the castle, Alex wished he could travel through time and find his bride.

"You need to relax, Alex." James crossed his arms. "Unburden yourself. I wish you would."

"You wouldnae believe a word I spoke should I." 'Twas past midnight and all were abed bar the guards who constantly patrolled the keep. Moonlight tinged the forest. No access could be gained on this side of the castle, the density of the bush as impenetrable as Dunvegan's stone walls. Even the guards didn't make regular rounds here because of it.

"I've never failed to believe you afore. Mother and Anne will recover. Is it no' a chill they suffer from?"

"Aye, a chill is all." He stroked the hilt of his ever-present claymore.

"Then what bothers you? You look prepared to battle, and far more than usual."

"We cannae remain here indefinitely." He couldn't continue to withhold from James. He'd share what he could, within reason.

"Aye, why would we wish to?"

"Neither can we sneak into Dunvegan without being seen."

"And again, why would we wish to?"

"I shall tell you what I can." Although nothing of Anne's time-travel. His brother would think him mad if he spoke of what he believed. Lowering his voice, he muttered, "Anne isnae here. Mother affects a sickness in order for us to stay."

His brother's bushy red brows drew together. "If Anne isnae here then why are we? How did she leave without anyone seeing her go?"

"I await her return because I fear this is the only place where she will. Anne is no' all she seems."

"Then what is she?"

"Anne is visiting a place far away. She had no choice but to go, and MacLeod wouldnae react well to the news of her travel should he find out."

"To where does she voyage? Why are you no' in pursuit?"

"To see her parents, I hope, although I'm no' entirely certain."

"You're saying we must wait for her return?" James scrubbed his jaw. "If Anne is able to slip in and out of the castle then why cannae we?"

Aye, a good question. "She takes a secret passageway and willnae speak of where it is. It's how she first left here and arrived at Dunscaith without a guard." He detested the lie, but he had no other choice.

"If she can sneak away at will, you need only leave word for her to follow us. Wait." His frown deepened. "Anne lost her parents some years ago. MacLeod is her rightful next of kin, correct?"

"Her parents live." Argh, mayhap he should never have tried to explain this to James.

"If that's the case, you should petition her father for this handfast, no' her chief."

"I wish it were that easy. If I could reach her father, I would ask his permission to wed her proper, but right now, I'll take what I can get."

"I see." James gripped his forearm. "I will stand by your side and aid you however I can."

"I know you will."

His brother clapped him on the back. "I'll check on Mother. Get some rest."

A thick ribbon of stars blanketed the black sky. He hadn't found that damn flag, but then Anne had wished upon it even though it had remained hidden. Mayhap that's all he needed to do too. He certainly required a little magic. Eyes closed, he whispered into the night, "I wish upon the Fairy Flag hidden within Dunvegan that the woman who holds my heart and all she loves, be permitted to travel back through time. Bring her home to me, so I might love her as my soul demands."

* * * *

Pushing a trolley loaded with suitcases, Anne's parents rounded the corner. Mum's golden hair, trimmed in a bob, was pinned on one side with a jeweled clip that sparkled in the sunlight streaming through the mass of windows surrounding them. Dad towered over her, his dark hair as thick as ever. He appeared far younger than his forty-five years, and shining from his eyes was a well of love as they met hers. They were alive, and they were here.

Arms open, she raced toward them, her heart near catapulting out of her chest. They swept her up, their arms banding around her like steel.

"We're together," Dad rumbled in her ear.

"And I never want to be parted from you again." She clung to them. "I love you."

"We love you too." Mum's tears mingled with hers. "It feels like forever since I've held you."

"It has been."

Beaming, Annie ducked around the roped partition. "Welcome home."

"Come here, Annie." Mum kissed her cheek then Annie's as she joined them. "Thank you for being here for Anne. Tor and I love you for it."

"It's as if we have two daughters, Morainne," Dad said.

"Yes, and they've both granted us the ultimate wish. Life and love returned."

Annie squeezed Anne's hand. "I'm so glad my wish led to this moment. I could never have envisioned this when I made it."

"Your wish led to far more than this moment." She hugged Annie back. "And if I could choose a sister, hands down it would be you. Right now, I can't even imagine having never met you."

"Sisters." Annie tightened her hold on her. "Forever."

"Deal." Anne gazed at her parents. "These past weeks I've learnt so much, to never give up, history can be changed, and that love should always prevail."

"Your mother and I are living proof it does. You've always been so tenacious. I shouldn't be surprised you've managed to travel back through time and do what you've done." Dad tweaked her chin. "Let's go home. We have so much to celebrate and catch up on.

"You've got it. Home."

Family was all that mattered, and she finally had hers back.

* * * *

Dad pulled into the driveway as the sun sank over the ocean horizon, yellow melding into dusky pink then inky-blue.

Mum gripped hers and Annie's hands and rushed them

133

inside. In the center of her kitchen, she twirled around. "Someone needs to pinch me."

"Allow me." Dad nipped Mum's cheeks. Oh, she'd missed seeing her parents together. She still had to keep pinching herself too, to make sure it was all real.

Mum nudged Dad toward the barstool. "Sit. I'm going to make dinner for us all and enjoy this moment.

"Please let me help." Annie patted the oven. "I'm fascinated by this woodless stove and need further instruction."

"We call it an oven." Mum laughed as she opened a drawer.

"Oven. Wonderful, that's what I'll call it too."

"You can be my sidekick, Annie." Mum flapped out an apron, looped it over Annie's head and tied it at the back. "Wait until I show you the beater which fluffs up the mashed potato. Now that is a miracle."

Mum adored her kitchen, and the house had always carried the scents of whatever she'd cooked or baked that day.

Anne couldn't wait for the evening meal. Her appetite had well and truly been restored with her returned parents. She plunked herself on the stool next to Dad. "Watch out, Annie. Being Mum's sidekick is a prime spot, but it means you'll have to do the dishes too."

"You shouldn't have warned her yet, Anne." Dad wrapped an arm around her shoulders. "And talking of sidekicks, you've yet to tell us of the man you handfasted with."

Hmm, she hadn't told them about the baby either. She hadn't wanted to mention it over the phone, or in the car, but now they needed to know. "Alex MacDonald leads his clan in his uncle's stead. From the moment I met him, I sensed a connection. I trusted him, felt safe and protected. We bonded quickly, as if somehow I'd already known him."

"Donald and William spoke to us. We know why you were hospitalized."

She squeezed his hand. "I'm sorry. I wanted to be the one to tell you and Mum."

Mum bustled around the countertop and hugged her. "It's okay, honey."

"I'm keeping Alex's child, Mum."

"I didn't expect anything less. Your baby will be greatly loved, by us all. Has your morning sickness eased?"

"I'm taking meds, and I'm much better."

"Good. I wish we could have met—oh, I clear forgot. All this talk about Alex has reminded me of his letter. How could I have forgotten? Annie, grab my purse from the table."

Annie snatched the red leather bag and passed it across. "Here you are."

Mum rummaged through then removed a red and white courier envelope and handed it to her. "Read it out loud. We can't have any secrets between us."

"I can't believe he wrote me." She clutched the thin package to her chest, her last lifeline to Alex. No, she had their child, the most precious gift ever. She glanced at her parents and Annie. Mum looked worried. Dad nodded encouragement, and Annie, her expression was full of sympathetic understanding. They were all here, and they'd never leave her.

"Open the letter." Mum nudged her then wrapped an arm around Annie's shoulders. "We're a family now, and we'll deal with what it says together."

"The most amazing family too." Annie nestled her cheek against Mum's shoulder.

"Okay, here I go." She unfolded Alex's letter and began.

"To the woman who holds my heart,

You just disappeared afore my eyes and I couldnae halt you from leaving.

Do whatever it takes, but damn well get back to me. You're no' raising our bairn alone.

Believe in us and wish your way back, as I will wish for

your return each and every day.
   I'll be waiting for you, always and forever.
   Alex."

She laid the letter on the countertop then traced the scrawled slash of his name. "I love him."

"He clearly feels the same way, and he needs you." Dad rubbed her hands between his. "No man wants to lose his family, not the way he has." He held out a hand to Mum and she tugged Annie with her and took it, then eyeing them all, he nodded. "Annie, your wish set in motion the most amazing event. And Anne, your drive and determination, and wishes as well, continued it. Girls, I want you to make another wish, one that will take all of us back through time. Our family isn't complete until we join Alex. My grandchild shall know its father."

"Dad, there's no telling what any wish Annie and I make might do. What if nothing happens? What it Annie alone is taken since she still remains outside of her time? What if she and I go and leave you and Mum behind?"

"So many what ifs. Remind me again what you've learnt these past weeks?"

"You can't expect me to take such a chance."

"I can and I do. At the airport you told us you've learnt to never give up, history can be changed, and love should always prevail. We have to try this."

"Yes." Mum nodded frantically. "We have to try this."

Annie gripped her other hand. "Anne, let's trust in our MacLeod fairy blood and all wish together. I've come from the past, you the future, and"—she eyed Morainne and Tor—"from far beyond either of those realms. Everyone has to wish with us."

"We'll all wish, Annie." Mum looked at Dad. "All of us."

"Yes, together."

"Okay, if you're all in then I'm in. Let's do this." Anne held her family.

"Aye, I'll begin." Annie cleared her throat. "I wish upon the Fairy Flag within Dunvegan Castle." They all repeated her words, unified as one. "That as kin, we shall travel back through time to where we most desire."

They chanted the wish, over and over.

Anne squeezed her eyes shut, wishing with all her heart to return to Alex, her heart's greatest desire.

"What are those lights?" Mum cried out.

Anne flung her eyes open. Stars surrounded them, blazing bright. Her hair whipped around her face and tangled in Dad's bristles as he pulled them ever closer.

"It's working," he laughed then suddenly sobered. "It's working."

"Annie." Her hold on her new sister was fierce. "Sisters forever."

"Forever," Annie whispered in awe. "We're going together, as we should." Wind tore around them. "No one let go," she yelled.

"Hold tight," Dad bellowed.

A mist rose and the stars blinked out.

Chapter 11

"Or mayhap more than a little magic." Atop the battlements, Alex opened his eyes. Stars flared and ebbed above in the night sky.

"Can you no' sleep, MacDonald?"

MacLeod. The man plagued him no matter where he was.

"Aye, mayhap you might help? A little exercise in the yard would aid me in bedding down better."

MacLeod stroked the dirk sheathed at his wrist. "Margaret should be abed and unable to interrupt us this—"

Light flashed out Anne's chamber window, so bright the courtyard glowed.

"What was that?" MacLeod gawked.

"Let me through." He shot past MacLeod who swiftly tore after him. Outside Anne's chamber, he pounded on the door.

"Coming." Margaret slung the door open then glanced between the two of them. "This is no' a good—"

"Out of the way, Margaret," MacLeod blared as he stormed in past Alex.

"Rory, nay."

Alex followed him into the chamber. The ruse was up, not that he'd expected it to—

From behind the bed curtains, a man dressed in well-pressed black trews and an impeccable blue shirt clambered out. The newcomer aided a woman to her feet. She wore a white silk dress, her flowing skirts embroidered with spring flowers along the hem. He'd never seen such clothing before.

A squeal came from the bed and two women scampered out and shoved their tangled, white-blond hair out of their eyes. They laughed and hugged each other. Anne. The other must be Annie. Was he seeing things?

"Annie?" Rory MacLeod regarded one woman then the other. "And another Annie? What in blazes is going on?"

"Rory." Annie engulfed him in a hug. "I've missed you."

He patted her back as he studied each of the others who'd arrived. "Who are these people?"

"I brought some guests. These are Anne's—"

"You brought guests? From where? I didnae see you leave, unless you took the secret—I mean, introduce them, and who is this woman who looks so alike you?"

"This is Anne MacLeod, and these are her parents, Tor and Morainne. They've traveled far to get here, although they've also come to visit Alex."

"I dinnae—" He shook his head. "But you two are—I must be seeing things."

"Nay. Anne and I are so similar because we're closely related. I first met Anne when I left here and traveled to Dunscaith. She joined me there. I'm afraid 'tis this Anne Alex handfasted with." She bit her lower lip. "Ah, I may have some explaining to do."

"Then begin." He crossed his arms.

"I didnae intend for Anne to have to handfast with Alex, but it happened all the same."

"You swapped positions with this Anne?" His look was incredulous.

"Aye, which is why I had to fix the problem I'd begun. This

illness I've had these past days was feigned in order to find Anne and her parents, and bring them here."

He glared at Margaret. "Why did you no' say?"

"I'm sorry, Rory." She gulped. "Annie's mind was made up, and the wrong had to be set right."

"Then who was it I fetched from MacDonald land?"

"That would be Anne." Annie gripped Rory's hands. "This is my fault. You must no' blame anyone other than me for what's happened."

"I'll blame whomever I wish, and you can be assured we'll discuss this later, and in far more depth." He eyed Tor. "I apologize for any inconvenience Annie has caused you and your kin. I'll see this matter rectified and ensure you're duly compensated."

"There's nothing to compensate. Annie is a delight, and we couldn't be more thrilled to be here." Tor extended his hand. "Call me Tor."

"Rory." He shook Tor's hand. "I shall still speak with her." He glowered at Annie. "Why are you wearing men's trews? Red trews?"

"Oh dear." She raced to the trunk, grabbed a plaid and wrapped it around herself.

Alex could no longer hold himself back. Anne was here, and her parents. The woman he'd longed to hold again stood a mere few feet away. "Anne, you're the one I handfasted with?"

She sashayed toward him, a vision in a pale yellow skirt and blouse. The sheer layers fluttered as she dipped into a curtsey. Rising, she winked. "Yes, and I apologize for my part in the deception." She motioned toward her kin. "This is my father, Tor, and my mother, Morainne. They've been eager to meet you."

"Yes, we have." Tor strode forward and offered him his hand. "My daughter tells me you two handfasted."

"Aye, at Dunscaith." He shook Tor's hand. "Sir, I hope you

will accept my invitation to travel there, and to stay as long as you wish."

"We'd like nothing more."

"Margaret." Annie tore across the chamber. "I've missed you."

Margaret hugged her and jiggled about. "What an adventure you must have had."

"I promise to tell you all about it. I've missed my favorite cousin too."

Anne looped her arm through Alex's. "Talking about adventures. I've had the greatest one of all. I'd love some fresh air and to discuss it with you. Do you mind?"

"Nay, come." He steered her out the door and upstairs to the battlements. He couldn't get her alone quick enough. In the dark, he pulled her into his arms. "I cannae believe you're here. And your parents."

"I have so much to tell you." She wound her arms around his neck. "I got your letter."

"There's something I must say first." Aye, it couldn't wait. His bride had returned and he had no intention of ever letting her go again. He lowered onto one knee.

"What are you—" She clapped a hand over her mouth.

"This is what I should have done from the beginning." He had to strengthen their bonds so no one could ever come between them again. He looked his fill of the woman who'd consumed his thoughts, from her golden hair gleaming in the moonlight to her high cheeks and sparkling blue eyes. "Anne MacLeod, I cannae live on this Earth without you. My love for you is unending and would weather any passage of time. I wish to take you as my wife, to bind you to me forever. Will you do me the great honor of marrying me?"

She dropped to her knees and clasped his face with shaky hands. "I love you too, more than my heart can stand. Yes, a hundred times over, yes."

"You'll never leave me again." He stood and swung her into his arms. He kissed her, allowing his hunger its ultimate release. She would be his, in this time and any other.

He had his woman back.

* * * *

"Okay, Alex, let's get one thing straight. I can walk. You didn't have to carry me down the steps." Alex set her down between him and the birlinn bobbing against the stone landing of Dunvegan's sea-gate. The new day had dawned, and the rising sun glimmered gold over the frothy waves rolling in. Even though chilly, the day was bright with wispy clouds streaming across the clear sky. A good day for sailing. "I'd also like to say goodbye to Annie and Margaret. To do that, I need you to move aside."

"The steps were slippery." Alex wrapped her more securely in his plaid. "And I've already invited Annie and Margaret to Dunscaith. You'll see them again soon."

"I'd like to see them now." She ducked under his arm. Men. Still, she understood why Alex had become so territorial since her return last night, but he'd have to let up a little, and soon.

Annie pulled her into her arms. "Margaret and I shall see you the moment we twist Rory's arm hard enough to allow the journey."

Rory grunted from beside Dad. Arms crossed, he nodded to her. "Safe travels, Anne. You and your parents are welcome to return whenever you wish."

Margaret joined hers and Annie's hug. "Take care and journey safely."

"I'll miss you both." She squeezed them so hard they groaned. Then it was her parents' turn. Mum held Annie close and promised her they'd visit her as well, and as often as they could.

Perhaps the feud had been set aside. Only time would truly tell. Regardless, she had her heart's desire. Her parents. Alex.

She couldn't wish for anything more.

"What are you thinking?" Alex lent her a hand and guided her into the birlinn. He seated her next to him on the wooden bench at the stern.

Her parents boarded and took a seat next to Mary. Alex's mother had missed their arrival last night and only caught up with all the happenings as they'd broken their fast. Mary too appeared eager to leave.

"Too much, yet not enough." She snuggled into Alex. "I'd like to see more of Scotland. You'll show me, won't you?"

"Whatever you wish, but within reason."

The men rowed, and James, aboard the other birlinn, sailed in tandem with them.

Together they left the seclusion of the loch and rounded the tip. Sails raised, they cruised south.

Alex lifted his face to the wind, his eyes closed as he breathed deep.

She did the same, taking in the scents of sea and Scotland's freshest air.

They stopped to rest during their trip as often as needed. This was the tour of her dreams, with her parents by her side.

They came ashore that night and the men set up camp, hunted game then roasted their meal over an open fire. She slept with Alex among their kin, sharing his plaid. Her heart expanded with love.

"Why are you no' asleep?" he murmured in her ear.

"I'm counting my blessings." She nuzzled into the small V at the neckline of his white linen shirt.

"Take care with how you touch me, love. A certain part of me has no' ceased aching since we left Dunvegan."

"Why didn't you say?" She swept her hand over the bulge in his trews. "Oh, that's got to be some ache."

He muttered several unrepeatable words.

"Come on. I'm going to ease your frustration right now, and

you're not going to argue otherwise." She pushed to her feet. "Take a walk with me."

"Nay, I can wait," he whispered madly.

"It doesn't appear so." She gripped his hand and tugged him until he stood.

"You are far too obstinate. We'll have to mind the guards." He ushered her around those sleeping and out of camp. Through the bush, he led her, until he slowly turned and nodded. "Aye, this is far enough." He spread his plaid under a tree. "Are you sure?"

"I'm a twenty-first century woman, and a very adventurous one at that. You never have to ask if I'm sure." She released the front laces of her amethyst gown. The cool night air skimmed over the exposed sliver of flesh.

"I'm quite taken with your adventurous nature." With painstaking slowness, he trailed his finger from between her breasts to her belly, his touch sending a torrent of delicious tingles spiraling out. "I cannae believe you're finally mine."

"I always have been." She eased her arms free of the long sleeves and the fabric slid down and bunched on her hips.

"Allow me." He lowered to his knees, planted his hands on her waist and pressed his lips to her belly. He kissed her where their child lay, the baby he would raise right along with her. "Your body is my body."

"Yours is mine too." She pushed her fingers deep into his thick blond hair and held onto him. "A body I'd really like to explore."

"Later. I wish a rediscovery first." He released the last fastening and her gown slithered to the ground. "Aye, I may even have new lands to discover."

"There's no—" She gasped as he widened her legs.

"Aye, the land of bounty." His voice was a purr as he licked the skin along her inner thighs. "'Tis every warrior's dream to find such a treasure."

She pressed her hips toward him and a thrill chased through her. He ducked his head and lashed her flesh with his tongue. Breathless, she clung to him, her heart soaring. "Slow down."

"Nay. A great prize awaits, one I wish to cherish and seek many times over."

He built her orgasm to a pinnacle until she tottered at the edge. "Alex."

"Give in to me, love."

She would love him forever, had crossed centuries to reach him, and she exploded, a brilliance of white and gold stars bursting behind her closed eyelids. Body and soul, her connection to him transcended time, and she came, over and over until she could take no more. His very scent become entrenched within her skin, their connection everything she'd ever desired, yet not nearly enough.

"Come inside me."

"The greatest jewel of all is your heart." Grinning, he tossed his shirt aside. His rippling abs and tanned pecs gleamed under the moonlight. Her warrior slid his trews down his muscular thighs and off. "I want to feel your heart beating against mine."

"It's racing a little out of time." Oh, good heavens. The man she loved was beyond beautiful, every hard and defined inch of him hers to explore and touch for all time.

"Good, just the way I like it." Naked, he scooped her up and lowered her onto his warm plaid. Lust filled his gaze as he rubbed his cock over her clit then plunged into her.

She bit back a scream as her inner muscles seized then pulled him in.

"I love you, Anne. From the depths of my soul all I have is yours." He covered her mouth with his and sent her body skyward again, but this time with him buried deep inside, right where he belonged.

Pleasure overflowed her, from the tips of her fingers to the ends of her toes. He rode her, hard, then kissed her senseless as he came right along with her.

"Ahh, so many riches, a cache I shall forever hoard." He kissed her, stroking her sides as he rocked gently inside her. With a tender touch, he slowly brought them both back down.

"I can't believe, were it not for Annie's wish, I would never have met you." She cupped his face between her hands, looked deep into his eyes. "I never want to be parted from you again."

"Nor I you." His cock twitched and lengthened again deep inside her. "It would seem I'm up for more exploration, but first, I fear I've neglected your beautiful breasts."

With infinite care, he embraced both mounds then nuzzled between them. "Aye, so full, and these sweet morsels—" He let out a husky moan as he drew her nipple deep into his mouth and sucked.

She closed her eyes, arched her back and enjoyed every moment of his loving.

Throughout the night, he lavished more attention on every single inch of her, and she returned the favor, finding her own booty within the plains of his body and plundering to her heart's desire.

It was the most magical night, and even though the first rays of dawn stole it from them, it was still only the first of many.

They rose in the morning and prepared to return to camp.

"Hold still while I dress you, love."

"I'll never get dressed with your wicked fingers continually sneaking in for a touch." She giggled then slapped his hands away. "I'll get these laces. You dress yourself."

With his molten gold eyes shimmering, he tucked in his shirttails.

"Not too fast, Alex. I'm enjoying the view."

"We have a full day of sailing ahead and I have yet to make you my wife." He shook out his plaid then wrapped it around himself. Secured with a leather girdle at his waist, he looked every lip-licking inch her Highland warrior.

"And when will that be?"

"Afore this day is out."

She nestled into his side as they returned, boarded their birlinn and finished their journey to Dunscaith, her Highlander's castle. This was where it had all begun.

Such a glorious sight. Light glowed from the narrow tower windows as dusk bathed the massive stone walls with a fiery gold.

They were home, and she was about to live the life she'd always dreamed.

Chapter 12

Sitting on the grassy hills surrounding Dunscaith, Anne relaxed against Alex's chest. She tucked her cobalt skirts under her legs as the waves crashed on the breeze.

Last night they'd spoken their vows before Brother John and their entire clan. She'd worn Mary's wedding dress a second time, and afterward, a feast had been held in their honor. Later, the night had been theirs, and today they lazed, enjoying being together, a freedom they'd fought so hard for.

"Can you hear that?" Alex played his fingers in her hair, surrounding her in his warmth.

"You mean my mother's laughter?" She shuffled forward. The land below sloped gently away, the lower meadow abloom with wildflowers. "Mary and Mum have baskets in hand. The castle shall be radiant on our return."

"I meant your father. James is working with him outside in the yard."

The warriors trained, although only half of them below, the other half swimming in the loch. James swung his sword, instructing Dad in the movements required. "He'll be in his element. Dad's always longed to take lessons with the sword. Men still wield those in the future, but in sport alone."

"I'll aid in his training as well. 'Tis no sport here. He'll need to become proficient in order to defend himself and those he loves in the Highlands." He eased back, taking her with him to lie flat in their hidden hollow.

She wrapped her arms around his neck as she wriggled on top of him. "Before you begin on him, I still need training."

"What would that be for?"

"For appreciating the fine wealth of flesh you've currently got covered."

"Aye, though 'tis you who wears far too many clothes." Grinning, he caressed her belly, holding her and their child close.

Intense emotions swamped her, the most wondrous love. It filled her heart to capacity. "I'll never let you go."

"I'll never allow it." He rolled her onto her back then kissed her, long and deep, and with infinite precision.

Every inch of her throbbed for more.

"I promise you forever, Alex."

"And I vow my eternal devotion. Let me begin your training, because I do recall you promised me a certain reward, one I intended to seek on our return from the hunt."

"Oooh, I love a good hunt."

Oh yes, and to have an abundance of time. Now with it returned to them, she allowed her love for him to overflow.

Love. Theirs had transcended time.

Author's Note

The ruins of Dunscaith Castle have always intrigued me, as well as the Highlander clans on the Isle of Skye. I chose to send Anne MacLeod back to the year fifteen-hundred and ninety, because Donald Gorme Mor MacDonald of Sleat, the Chief of Clan MacDonald at this time, had been imprisoned by the king due to his feud with the MacLean of Duart. The king did in fact induce all those involved in the dispute, being Donald MacDonald of Sleat, Angus MacDonald of Dunnyveg and Lachlan MacLean of Duart, to go to Edinburgh. When they each arrived, they were apprehended and imprisoned. I altered this event slightly, allowing for MacDonald's capture by the king's men to suit the story. His successor was his nephew Donald MacDonald, a minor, and with someone needing to lead the clan, I chose Alex.

Alex MacDonald, Anne and Annie McLeod are fictional characters.

Sir Roderick Ruairidh Mor MacLeod, the fifteenth Chief of Clan MacLeod, was known as Rory, and Margaret was his younger sister.

The Fairy Flag belonging to clan MacLeod does hang within a frame in the great hall of Dunvegan Castle, although it's now merely a thin piece of fabric.

This story is woven with as much accuracy to the period and locations as possible, but any mistakes made are mine alone.

This book forms part of my *Highlander Heat* series, and each within it are stand-alone.

Please feel free to search for any of my other works. I simply adore strong heroines, and have a ton of fun matching them with their honorable alpha heroes.

**Also available in paperback
Scottish Historical Romance**

Traveling through time…for a Highlander.

Highlander Heat Series

Highlander's Castle, Book One

Highlander's Magic, Book Two

Highlander's Charm, Book Three

Highlander's Guardian, Book Four

Highlander's Faerie, Book Five

Highlander's Champion, Book Six

by Joanne Wadsworth

Looking for more sexy Scottish adventure?

Read on to catch a preview of the next book in the
Highlander Heat series.

Highlander's Magic

Highlander Heat Book Two

by Joanne Wadsworth

Highlander's Magic

Highlander Heat Series, Book Two

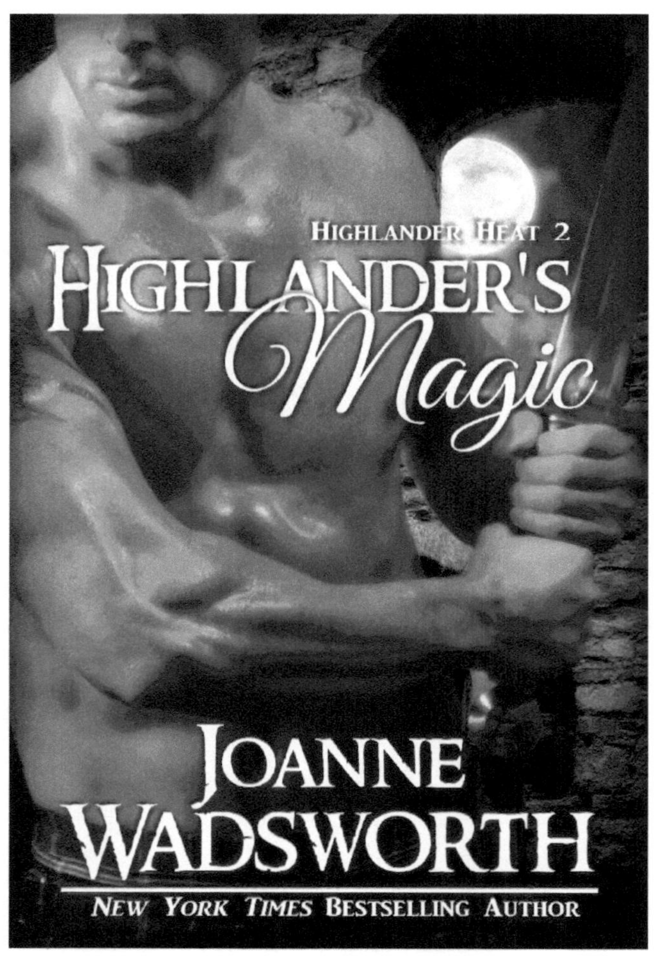

Chapter 1

The ruins of Dunyvaig Castle, on the Isle of Islay, Scotland.

"I can't believe these ruins were once the home of Mum's MacDonald ancestors." Marie MacLean belted her white woolen coat tighter. Dunyvaig Castle had stood guard over this sought after entrance of Lagavulin Bay, when a powerful stronghold and sea base meant the difference between life and death.

"Clan MacDonald ruled Islay centuries ago." Katherine, her twin, flapped her tour brochure open where they stood high on the craggy rise. "Yet Dad's clan MacLean ancestors continually feuded with them from the nearby isles. We're like the progeny of two bickering clans who knew very little peace."

"What about poor Mary?" Marie rubbed the silver amulet at her neck. The MacDonald clan crest was engraved on one side, and on the reverse, the MacLean's crest. "The two clans should have come together in harmony the day Mary MacLean wed the MacDonald chief. Instead the feud became bitterer."

"Does the feud intrigue you because of Mary's gift?"

"Absolutely. Mary bequeathed this amulet to her eldest daughter requesting it be passed down through the generations until it once again came into the possession of a MacLean. That took over four-hundred years. It's as if Mary is trying to send me a message, only I've no idea what."

"And you're definitely the eldest daughter of both a MacDonald and a MacLean, Marie. She wanted you to have her amulet."

"Yes, but what am I supposed to do with it?" She hadn't removed Mary's gift since receiving it a few months ago on her twenty-first birthday. Mere weeks before Mum lost her battle with cancer, she'd placed it around her neck. Mum's final wish had been for her and Katherine to bring the amulet home to Dunyvaig Castle as Mary had requested. So halfway around the world they'd traveled, from Australia's Gold Coast, and then by ferry from Scotland's mainland to this isle.

Such a rugged, yet beautiful land. Marie lifted her face toward the sky. It would be even more picturesque if the heavy gray clouds above diffused. "It looks like we're in for some bad weather."

"A storm I'd say. It's strange how their seasons are in the reverse to ours. It's autumn here, while Down Under we left spring behind. Everything feels off kilter." Katherine ambled into Dunyvaig's faerie circle and sat on the center stone. The tartan red and blue of her woolen coat made her a bright beacon of color. "Come and sit with me."

Marie perched on the edge of the large flat stone. "Why are we sitting when we should be exploring?"

"Because I'm going to help you figure out what to do with Mary's amulet."

"I wish Mary had left more precise instructions."

"Well, Mum said we had to—" Katherine blinked furiously, suddenly fighting tears.

They talked about Mum all the time, but grief still consumed them. She'd been forty-five. In the prime of her life.

Katherine scrubbed a hand over her face, composing herself. "I'm sorry. I miss Mum so much. This would've been the trip of a lifetime for her."

"Which is why we promised her we'd come. We're going to live her dreams for her. At least we get to do this together." She hugged Katherine, and her sister's sweet vanilla scent, the same as what their mother had worn, soothed her. It wasn't fair they'd lost both their parents. Dad a year past, and now Mum. It was only her and Katherine.

"Promise me you'll never leave me like they did." Katherine squeezed her back.

"I promise. I love you." Her sister was her life.

"I love you too." Katherine let out a long breath. "So, back to amulet. You brought it here to Dunyvaig. We can check off that request."

"The first and only request following the bestowment. Hmm, maybe if we look around I might have an epiphany." This place was so remote with its grassy moors rolling for miles in both directions.

"Good idea. Let's do that. This faerie circle is pretty amazing. Let me take a picture of us before we leave it." Katherine lugged her cell phone from her jeans pocket and readied it for a shot. "Get closer, sis."

She flattened her cheek to Katherine's and smiled. Throughout their lives, they'd done everything together, and this was yet another adventure.

"Smile." Katherine clicked and checked the picture. "Mirror images. I could've just taken a photo of me and not worried about you."

"You say that all the time." She knocked her shoulder against Katherine's, rose and wandered inside the circle. "I wonder how the faeries got these stones here. They're massive." Nine six-foot high stones stood six feet apart around the perimeter. A tenth stone, short enough to sit on but still as wide, sat plumb in the center. "What else does the brochure say about this circle, other than it's sacred?"

"Just to watch for changes within. It can go from still to wildly windy, but most of all, if a haze surrounds it, the faeries are at play."

"A haze? You mean like—"

Thunder rumbled out at sea, and birds nesting along the rocky shoreline cackled and took flight. Their wings brushed the water as they flew across the inlet to the rushes hugging the other side's marshy edge.

"Bad weather is getting closer, Marie. Maybe we should come back and explore tomorrow." Her sister stood.

"We can give it more time. If need be, we'll make a mad dash to the car. This is a magical circle. Perhaps we could simply wish for fine weather."

"Wishes shouldn't be squandered on weather." A gleam lit Katherine's eyes. "If we're going to make one, it has to be interesting."

Katherine had always loved to make wishes, by the first star she saw at night, to blowing out her birthday candles, to when she lost an eyelash. She'd never been able to stop her sister from making them.

"Come on." Katherine gripped her hands. "I'll make a wish for something both of us have always wanted."

"I'd like an endless supply of chocolate." That would be fabulous.

Katherine chuckled. "Yeah, we can buy chocolate anytime. How about an endless supply of adventure? You can't always buy that."

"Sure. It's why we're here."

"Great." Katherine winked. "Then here's my wish. To the faerie folk of Dunyvaig Castle, I wish for a moment of magic, for Marie and me to live, for us to have untold adventure on your stunning isle. Bring on the fun. Bring on the—"

Thunder boomed and lightning slashed the rippling waves of the bay with a sizzling crackle.

"Okay, I think a mad dash is now in order." She lugged Katherine toward the edge of the circle, hit a hazy barrier and bounced to the ground. "Ouch." She rubbed her nose. "Where'd that come from?"

"Whoa." Gaping, Katherine hauled her to her feet. "It's like a veil's come down."

"You mean you weren't joking when you mentioned the haze?" Beyond the fog, the darkening waves rolled in with a pounding crash.

"This can't be right." Katherine inched forward and patted the sides. "Except there's really something here. How do we get out?"

"Try the other side." This place already spoke of mystery and intrigue, and now it had ramped right up.

"I thought the brochure was simply playing up the whole mystical fae thing." Katherine tapped around the perimeter, knocking on something solid, yet nothing but foggy air swirled. She shot her a wide-eyed look. "Obviously not, and I just made a wish."

"There's got to be a way out. Even if we have to dig, we'll find it." Marie grabbed her sister's hand. Low cloud lit with lightning coasted across the sea. Within the mist a vessel materialized, one reminiscent of a sixteenth century Highland birlinn. "Do you see that, sis? Or is my imagination really going wild?"

Katherine gasped. "A-are those warriors onboard that thing?"

Thirty or so armed men wearing green and blue plaids plunged their oars into the sea and powered their vessel in. At the helm, a commanding man pumped his fist into the air and bellowed orders for his men to lower the sail.

"I…um…I'd say so."

"They're heading right toward us." Katherine pressed her palms against the barrier. "I think my wish just got a whole lot more adventurous than I expected."

"Y-yeah, you're banned now from making—look at the ruins." The manned birlinn now appeared to be the least of her and Katherine's problems. "You see the castle, right?"

Her sister gawked past the clingy mist. "Holy moly. Birlinns. Warriors. Do you think we just fell back through time?"

"Either that or the locals play out reenactments, of an incredibly spectacular sort." She scrubbed her eyes with her knuckles, but the castle remained, standing three stories high on the hill. Battlements topped fortified walls, and candles lit tower windows. In the descending dark, the castle guarded the bay like a sentinel.

"'Tis our captain, Archie MacDonald," a guardsmen called as he rushed along the top of the barbican. This was too real to be a reenactment. No one could rebuild a castle in seconds.

A portcullis rose from within the stone-arched entrance gate, its clunky chains reverberating across the moors. Boots clipped loudly on the stones as a warrior strode out in leather pants and a thick fur vest over a dark linen shirt. He halted at the edge of their circle. "Prepare the great hall for our men's arrival." He palmed the hilt of the sword at his side. "My brother returns."

Marie waved her hand in front of the warrior. "Okay, he can't see us but we can see him. We must be between times, protected somehow by the veil."

"Here, but not here." Katherine glanced at the bay. "Those men are huge. Look at the size of them."

Talk about intimidating. Highlanders, and clearly born of Vikings. Onboard, the men slashed their oars in the reverse direction and slowed their vessel. It skimmed the water as it cruised to the sea-gate. With another booming command from the captain, two of the men leaped into the waist-deep water, seized the bow and roped it to a catch alongside the stone landing.

One by one, they disembarked, jogged up the trail and disappeared into the keep. The captain followed, veering toward the warrior standing before them. "John, is all well?"

"Well enough. Welcome home, Archie." John grasped the captain's shoulders. "Do you have any further word on the chief?"

"I have but 'tis no' good. The king's men have apprehended Angus, as well as his brother, Donald MacDonald of Sleat. I spoke with Donald's second at Dunscaith Castle afore I traveled to Edinburgh."

"You've been all the way to see the king?"

"Aye. Angus is being kept under strict guard, in the highest level of the tower. He and Donald have their own chambers. They're together, yet isolated from the other prisoners." He paced, displaying a massive two-handed claymore holstered to his broad back.

A warrior born to fight, wearing a great plaid secured over his chest with a silver pin and belted low at his waist with a leather girdle. She surely wouldn't mind meeting a man like—oh, what was she thinking? Admiring a man when she and Katherine were trapped like this. Where was her head?

Archie stopped, planted his feet wide. "There isnae any way to rescue him, or at least no' since our arrival raised suspicion and the number of guards increased. I left after being permitted a short conversation with him."

"What did he say? Why was he taken?"

"Angus spoke of a missive he received from the king requesting he present himself at court to atone for his feuding with Mary's brother, the MacLean of Duart. The missive had gone to all three chiefs involved in the feud, including Donald. Angus had no intention of presenting himself, but seeking further counsel with his brother when he made the trip to Skye. The king's men caught him. Donald as well."

"Hell, the king needs to leave us alone to resolve our own

issues, no' alter the way we settle our disputes. He clearly wishes to stamp his mark of ownership on the isles, to control us as he does the rest of Scotland." John clenched his fists. "Angus should have taken more care. Mary is so close to giving birth."

"There's naught we can do about Angus, no' since the king will have his way. Angus said the king is after a settlement, but without Lachlan MacLean, naught can be conferred. I say 'tis better MacLean be removed from the discussions. Angus believes so too. He instructed me to see to MacLean's death, ensuring the king no longer has a reason to hold either him or his brother."

Marie grabbed Katherine. "He must be talking about Mary after she wed Angus MacDonald. We must have arrived at some point in the late 1500s."

"That'd make sense since you're wearing Mary's amulet from that time and this circle brought us here. Do you recall anything about the king capturing Angus and Donald MacDonald because of the feud? I didn't read up like you did before we came."

"I do. All three chiefs involved were taken, but I'm not sure how long they were held. Mary must be here somewhere." Incredibly, history was unfolding before her eyes. "Archie certainly can't kill MacLean as he's said though. If he did, he'd alter history. The king wished an intervention, and all three chiefs entered the discussion." Damn, she couldn't recall if the talks had helped though.

"We're in a different time, sis. History has yet to occur. Maybe we've been brought here for a reason. This has to have something to do with your—"

"There's a haze over the circle this eve." Archie rubbed the towering stone nearest Marie. "Mayhap a touch of faerie magic wouldnae go amiss in winning this war against MacLean. He has to die."

John stepped in beside Archie. "It does appear the faerie

folk are at play."

Mischievous imps for sure. These two warriors didn't know the half of it.

Archie pressed his palm against the veil. His shoulder-length brown hair wisped with blond fluttered in the night breeze. Marie edged closer to him. Gorgeous, if a warrior could be called such. His chin, sharply defined with a deep cleft in the center, held rugged appeal, and his eyes were a stunning shade of molten gold. She might drown in those liquid depths. "Archie, don't make that wish and change history," she murmured. "MacLean can't die. It's not his time."

"Did you hear that?" Archie frowned, shaking his head. "I swear I heard something. Whispers from within. Mayhap the faerie folk wish to aid us. We certainly cannae become vulnerable to an attack should MacLean take this opportunity to stake his revenge. Word will soon spread of Angus and Donald's capture, if it has no' already."

"No. I said MacLean can't die. Don't do it." She pressed her hand against the barrier an inch from the warrior's hand. Electricity buzzed through her, raising the hairs on her arms in a delicious, tingly way. She tried to inch closer.

Katherine eyed John across from her and pressed against the veil nearest him. "Maybe this is why Mary wished for the amulet to return home. Maybe she needed help and asked the fae for aid."

"Do you really think so?" If her sister was right, untold adventure was on its way.

"Why else are we here? Fae magic brought us back through time. This isn't a reenactment."

"I know, but what should we do?" Marie edged closer to Archie.

"The whispers grow stronger, brother. Magic hums in the air." Archie's gaze narrowed on her as he searched within.

"Aye, make your wish while I find Mary. I dinnae want her

hearing of Angus's capture afore I can speak to her. The men will be hard-pressed to delay her questioning."

"Go. I'll be with you shortly."

John strode off into the dark.

"Aye, the air vibrates far too strongly no' to state my desire." Archie rubbed the veil. "Guardians of Dunyvaig, I ask for a wish. I seek my chief's return and require your aid in this journey. Send me a sign. I must win this war against MacLean."

The veil shimmered and Marie's pulse spiked. "I can almost touch him, sis. The haze is thinning."

"Marie, I think you should step back," her sister warned.

"Marie?" Archie whispered her name. "The faeries have given me a name."

"He heard you, Katherine." Marie pushed toward him. "I have to warn him not to kill MacLean."

"Come to me, Marie. Mayhap you are the sign." His husky words swarmed her senses as he swept his hand through the air.

Her amulet rose, breached the barrier between them and spun into his palm. She'd tell him in person.

"Wait!" Katherine yanked her coat. "You're not going anywhere without me."

"Hold onto me. He needs us." Wind tunneled around her, whipping her hair across her face.

"Come, my faerie." Archie jerked her amulet.

"Whoa." She lurched through the barrier and slammed into the warrior. His body was solid, his flesh warm and his hold tight.

"Unbelievable." His gaze searched hers. "A faerie in truth. My sign, as I wished."

"I—I—"

The circle was again thick with the haze. But where was Katherine? She should have come with her. She pounded the veil. "Hey, I said to hold on, sis. I don't want to do this on my own. Get here now, or you're going to be in a ton of trouble."

* * * *

Afraid the faerie would get away, Archie gripped her arm as she called out for another. She had a strange accent, like the Lowlanders. "Who is Katherine?"

"My sister. She was right there with me in the circle."

"There is none here but you and me." The faerie's white-blond hair shimmered to her waist, and her eyes shone the deepest shade of midnight-blue. He stroked the soft folds of her white woolen coat. Never had he known such a fine weave. Her legs were covered in white linen, clothing similar to men's trews yet completely feminine. White knee-high leather boots encased her feet. Head to toe, a vision.

'Twas a powerful circle to deliver one holding such magic. The power radiating from this circle had beckoned him time and again over the years. The faeries often played, throwing up a haze or causing the wind to sweep through or become completely still. Now it had brought him her. "Mayhap your sister will come another time?"

"She has to come now. Her wish was for both of us." She struggled to push back in. "I can't leave her behind."

"The veil is strong. I've never been able to pass through when it's risen." He shoved his upper arm against it. "When the haze is gone, you can enter, though none do. 'Tis a sacred place, and now with my wish, the fae have delivered you. Your sister must no' be needed."

"Of course she's needed, and I didn't mean to answer your wish without my sister."

"What does your sister look like?"

"We're identical twins." She grasped his shirt. "I really can't leave her behind. I've got to get back in."

"You dinnae appear to have a choice, otherwise she would have come, or you would have been able to return." Aye, she was here to stay, this faerie with her tiny nose and high cheeks sprinkled with freckles. So young and enchanting. Never had a faerie graced one of his clan with their presence like this. They tinkered and played, but they also guarded their lands, having ensured Dunyvaig never fell into MacLean's hands. "Magic has brought you to me when we need it the most. I have a war to win, and you're a wonder bestowed by the circle. You even wear Mary's amulet. How did you come by it?"

She gripped the piece. "I'm no faerie, just a regular person, and Mary gifted this to me. She left instructions asking I return it to Islay."

"Good. Then you have done as she asked." He cupped her cheek. "Fae you are, your presence one of magic." 'Twas abundantly clear, and she would never convince him otherwise.

"I'm not from this time or place."

"Aye, you've come from your own time and place. The fae live—"

"I didn't mean it that way. I'm really not one of the fae." She glared at the veil then slammed her hands against it. "This is impossible. Guardians of Dunyvaig, I wish to be reunited with Katherine. Send her through, or let me back in. Please, do something."

"Nay, lass. You must stay. See to my wish and then you may go. The guardians willnae keep you here beyond the time you've been sent. I'm certain of it."

"How long will this barrier be up for?"

"It comes and goes, depending on your people."

"The fae aren't my people."

"Aid me, and I promise you my protection." It appeared his faerie didn't wish to accept her destiny. He would convince her otherwise. "No harm shall ever come to you. My word is true."

"My sister and I never do anything without each other."

"Mayhap this is the one time you shall."

"Excuse me, but I'd rather not." Arms crossed, she thumped her foot. "You really don't listen very well."

A woman with fire. Even better. She would need to be

strong in order to grant him his wish. He had a battle ahead of him against MacLean, and the Chief of Duart was no easy adversary. "What would your sister wish you to do right now?"

"Return to her." She huffed then slid Mary's talisman over her head. "Or return to her the moment I'd seen to your wish. Katherine is the adventurous sort. She's probably peeved she's not here right now, as well as freaking out about being alone. I've got to get back to her, and since this talisman brought me here, hopefully it will do the same and bring my sister to me."

"Your words are strange. 'Tis clear you speak of another world."

"No, this world, just a different time." She stepped back then frowned. "Hold on. The veil's lifting."

"Then be quick about what you need to do to bring your sister through. Throw her the amulet afore the veil disperses."

She tossed the talisman and it landed with a clunk on the center stone. "Take the amulet, Katherine. Mary may have bequeathed it to me, but use it to get out as I did." She fanned her hand through the veil as it continued to thin. "Please, hurry."

It shimmered and vanished on the wind, gone as quick as it came. "Lass, the fae are nay more, but they always return. You must now wait."

"No, this can't be happening. I need my sister." She staggered inside and fell to her knees before the center stone. "Katherine, come back."

His heart heaved for her loss, but it wouldn't be for long. "You've come for a reason, Marie. To aid me." He held out his hand. "Come. I shall look after you as I promised."

"I didn't want to do this alone."

"Once you've fulfilled my wish, you can return. I didnae ask for any more than your aid. Come."

She swiped her tears then rose and wobbled toward him. "If I help you, it's because I want to get back to Katherine."

"Aye, lass." A few more steps and she cleared the circle. He caught her around the waist and held her close. His faerie would aid him, just as he needed her to. "Together we cannae fail against MacLean. You'll soon be back with your sister."

"Since I don't have any other choice, tell me where to start. The sooner I'm done here, the sooner I can return."

"'Tis late and I've traveled far this day. We'll begin on the morrow. For now, you're welcome to use my chamber to rest. It overlooks this circle, which should bring you comfort."

"Are you taking me inside?" Her beautiful eyes widened as she glanced at the castle.

"You've naught to fear." Eager to get her within the safety of the Dunyvaig's walls, he tugged her under the arched entrance. "No one would ever harm one of the fae."

Within the inner courtyard, stone buildings rose all around them. He steered Marie up the side stairs, bypassing the great hall where his clan had gathered for the evening meal. Inside his chamber on the third floor, he ushered her in and shut the door.

She hurried to the window, shoved open the wooden shutters and peered through the dark. "I can see the circle, just." She slumped against the stone sill. "I can't believe I've left Katherine behind. It all happened so fast."

"Believe it, lass." He crossed to the fireplace, lit and stoked it into life. It blazed and spread its heat through the room. After taking a candle and lighting it from the flames, he set in in the corner stand next to his bed. The warmth and light should soothe her.

"Please, tell me more about the circle." Her gaze remained glued to it.

"There is never an assurance of when the veil rises, only that it does." He eased in behind her. The stones, lit by the moonlight, appeared ghostly white, and Mary's talisman sparkled atop the center stone. "As no one enters the circle, the amulet will remain within should your sister have need of it."

"Yes, I don't want anyone moving it." She peered at him.

"And it used to be Mary's talisman. I know you don't believe me, but I've told you the truth. She gifted it to me on my twenty-first birthday."

"'Tis impossible."

"I've no reason to lie." She shook her head. "I'll convince you somehow. First, tell me more about the warrior with you before. John. You called him your brother. Could he keep a watch out for my sister? The more who do, the better."

"John is my twin. We are similar but no' identical, and aye, I will have him and the guards keep an eye out. As soon as you're comfortable, I'll go speak with him." If reassurance was what she needed, he could easily provide it.

* * * *

"Yes, speak to him, please. That's what I want." Marie clutched Archie's arm. She would have to see to his wish, which had better not take long. Katherine needed her, would be so worried.

"First, tell me more about your sister." He stroked her back, his touch sending a delicious tingle to her toes. "You said her wish was for both of you. What was it she asked for?"

"For a moment of magic. She wished for us to live and to have untold adventure along the way, although I doubt she meant quite this much adventure." Never this much.

"Will anyone other than her miss your presence?"

"No. Our mother, Marianne MacDonald, passed away a few months ago. Our father, Locky MacLean, the year before." He thought her fae and she had to set him right. Convincing him she was from the twenty-first century wouldn't be an easy task, but she had to try. "I don't want there to be anything but the truth between us. I'm from a time far in the future, and I'm a direct descendent of Mary's, well Mary and Angus's on my mother's side. The amulet I wore was Mary's. I received the family heirloom in my time, through my maternal line. Mary left instructions it be handed from her eldest daughter to her eldest daughter until it once again came into the possession of a daughter born to a MacLean. That's me."

"Angus and Mary's bairns are too young. What you speak of isnae possible."

"You have to keep an open mind. I truly am both MacDonald and MacLean. My name is Marie MacLean. I've traveled here from the year two-thousand and fourteen." She couldn't state it more clearly.

"Nay, lass. There's no need to ply your tricks. Fae you are, and fae you remain." Clicking his tongue as if in admonishment, he strode to the door. "I'll ask a servant to bring a tray. Make yourself comfortable while I speak with John."

"I'm really not fae." She raced after him, snatched his arm. "You have to believe me."

He tweaked her chin. "'Tis the year fifteen-hundred and ninety. Now, no more. On the morrow, you'll work your magic. MacLean must be halted." He closed the paneled door with a thunk. Gone.

Hopefully it didn't matter if he believed her or not, but she'd rather he did. His disbelief didn't change the fact she was now in Scotland though, somewhere far in the past and needed to fulfill his wish before she could return to Katherine.

She stalked to the window, needing to be closer to Katherine even though currently impossible. She'd tried to learn all she could about Mary MacDonald before she'd traveled here, but with over four-hundred years passing, the information had been sparse. More was recorded on her husband, Angus MacDonald, and brother, Lachlan MacLean, both chiefs of their own clans. Although, she'd never quite understood how the intense feud had begun.

Right now, she'd try to seek the answers she needed, and from Mary no less. The task before her was immense. Aid Archie in winning the war, while ensuring he didn't change history and kill MacLean.

Her sister's wish would certainly provide a ton of adventure, and with her own Highland warrior on the side.

But she'd do whatever it took to ensure she returned.

There was no other option.

Katherine needed her, and she needed Katherine.

Highlander Heat

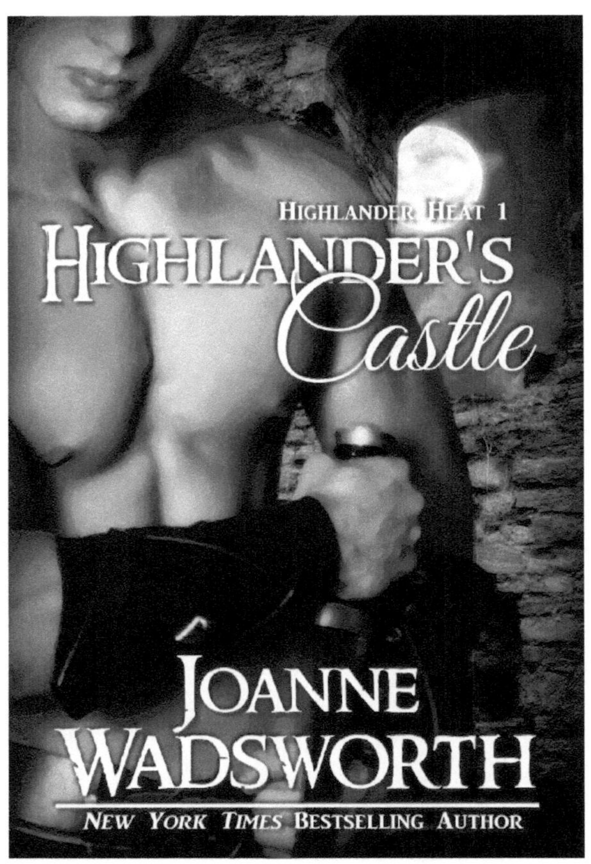

Regency Brides

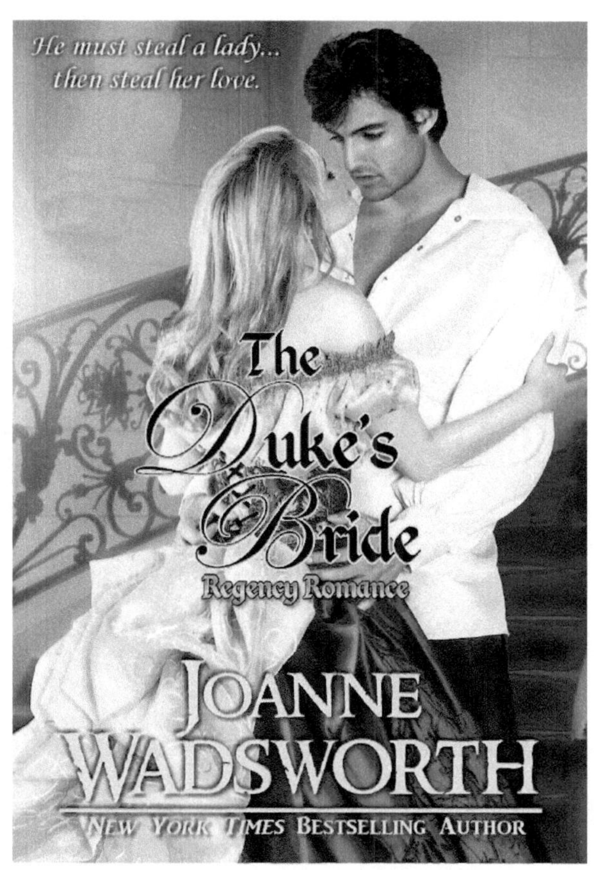

The Matheson Brothers Continued

Highlander's Kiss, Book Four
Highlander's Heart, Book Five
Highlander's Sword, Book Six

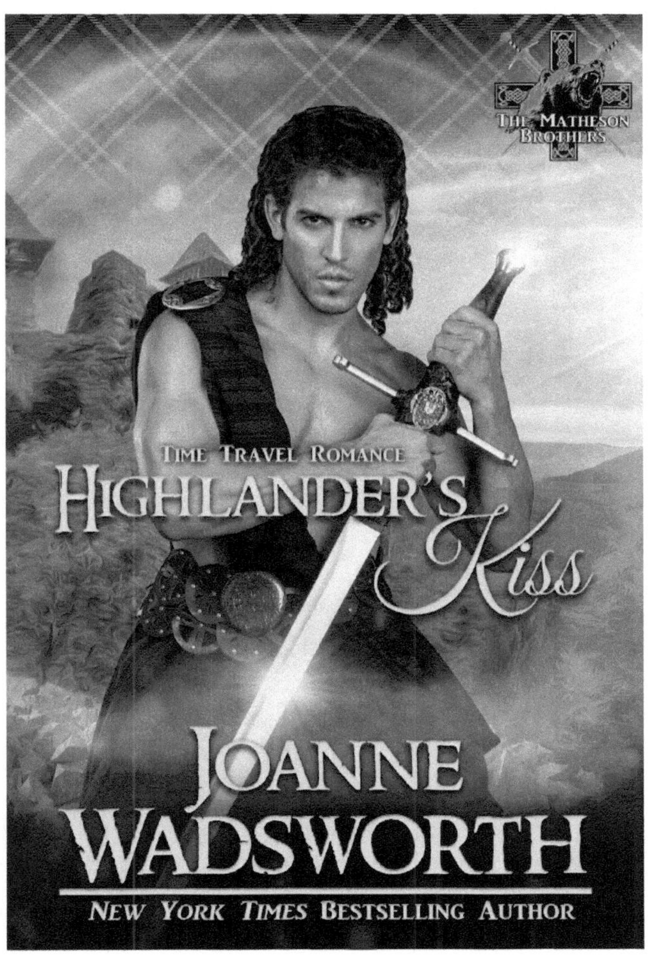

The Matheson Brothers Continued

Highlander's Bride, Book Seven
Highlander's Caress, Book Eight
Highlander's Touch, Book Nine

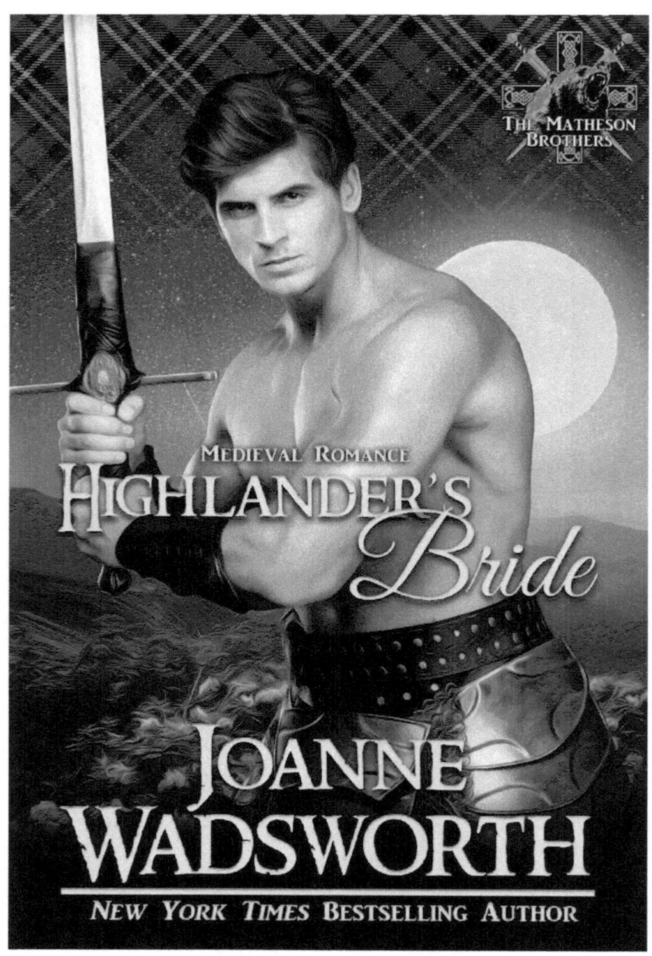

The Matheson Brothers Continued

Highlander's Shifter, Book Ten
Highlander's Claim, Book Eleven
Highlander's Courage, Book Twelve
Highlander's Mermaid, Book Thirteen

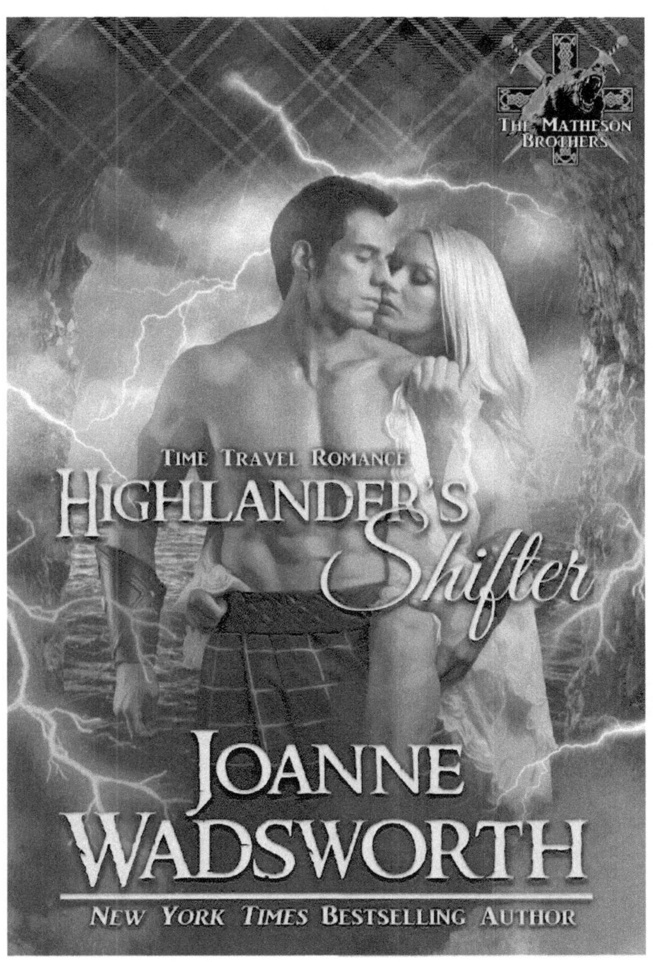

Princesses of Myth

Protector, Book One
Warrior, Book Two
Hunter (Short Story - Included in Warrior, Book Two)
Enchanter, Book Three
Healer, Book Four
Chaser, Book Five

Billionaire Bodyguards

Billionaire Bodyguard Attraction, Book One
Billionaire Bodyguard Boss, Book Two
Billionaire Bodyguard Fling, Book Three

JOANNE WADSWORTH

Joanne Wadsworth is a *New York Times* and *USA Today* Bestselling Author who adores getting lost in the world of romance, no matter what era in time that might be. Hot alpha Highlanders hound her, demanding their stories are told and she's devoted to ensuring they meet their match, whether that be with a feisty lass from the present or far in the past.

Living on a tiny island at the bottom of the world, she calls New Zealand home. Big-dreamer, hoarder of chocolate, and addicted to juicy watermelons since the age of five, she chases after her four energetic children and has her own hunky hubby on the side.

So come and join in all the fun, because this kiwi girl promises to give you her "Hot-Highlander" oath, to bring you a heart-pounding, sexy adventure from the moment you turn the first page. This is where romance meets fantasy and adventure…

To learn more about Joanne and her works, visit
http://www.joannewadsworth.com